BEAR RAZED

ALPHA GUARDIANS - BOOK 5

KAYLA GABRIEL

GET A FREE BOOK!

JOIN MY MAILING LIST TO BE THE FIRST TO KNOW OF NEW RELEASES, FREE BOOKS, SPECIAL PRICES AND OTHER AUTHOR GIVEAWAYS.

http://freeshifterromance.com

Bear Razed: Copyright © 2018 by Kayla Gabriel

ISBN: 978-1-7959-0216-8

All Rights Reserved. No part of this book may be reproduced or transmitted in any form or by any means, electrical, digital or mechanical including but not limited to photocopying, recording, scanning or by any type of data storage and retrieval system without express, written permission from the author.

Published by Kayla Gabriel
Gabriel, Kayla
Bear Razed

Cover design copyright 2018 by Kayla Gabriel, Author

Images/Photo Credit: Fotolia

This book has been previously published.

AN EXCERPT

"What if… what if I want both of you?" she asked, her voice so quiet that Kieran almost lost it in the pounding beat of the music. She ducked her head a little, as if ashamed of her own appetite.

Kellan glanced up at Kieran for the barest moment, a look full of a hundred tiny thoughts. Kieran only nodded, knowing what Kellan was thinking.

Sera wouldn't be the first woman they'd shared in this way, at the same time…

Kieran pulled Sera onto his lap even as Kellan surged forward, kissing her deeply, digging his fingers into her hair. Sera went rigid against Kieran for the briefest second, then surrendered with a moan. Kieran pulled her hair back and teased her earlobe with his lips, chuckling when one of her hands clutched at his knee, nails digging into his skin through his jeans.

Yes, sweet little Sera was already quite perfect. Like she was made for this, made for both of them.

If only that were possible…

PROLOGUE

THE FAERIE REALM

Long, long ago

Kellan stood before the great wild throne of his Aunt Maeve, his chest heaving with the exertion of not launching himself at her, attacking the new Queen outright. She sat on the throne, her elegant white-blonde hair piled high on her head, her blood-red dress pushing her lovely breasts up toward her face, two dark spots of blush painted on her cheeks. She considered Kellan for a long moment, running her tongue over the deep red of her berry-tinged lower lip. She was so exquisite, one could almost forget all she'd done. Or the silver dagger that she held in one hand, running a fingertip over a blade as sharp as her cunning smile.

Her pale green eyes gleamed with excitement, which only riled Kellan up more. He wanted her *dead*. It seemed an impossible thing, two teenaged Princes against the mighty

Faerie Queen, but he longed for it more than he could ever say.

His fists were clenched so hard that his fingers were nearly numb as he stared at the verdant grasses and slithering vines of the Queen's throne. He glanced around the moonlit forest clearing that served as a throne room and looked at the beautiful, shining Fae gathered to watch the events, every shape, size, and shade of seductive loveliness. Anything to keep himself from staring right into Maeve's emerald eyes, for he couldn't begin to hide the gleam of murderous intent that would be found there by anyone who knew him well.

He knew this, because his twin brother Kieran was only a dozen paces away, wearing that exact same expression and not making any attempt to hide it. Already, the other Faeries slowly drew near, sensing conflict in the air. Kieran, ever the Dark one, ever the outcast… he would bring down Maeve's anger, it was clear as the tolling of a bell to all present.

The tall, ethereal Fae of the Seelie Court were beautiful, but their looks were all smoke and mirrors, glamour used to impress and flatter others. With their shapely bodies, dark eyes, and light skin, their looks were every bit as misleading at that of the dark, frightening Fae in the Unseelie Court. Both kinds of Faerie could be kind and vicious at turns.

And right now, the Fae 0f the Summer Court could sense blood in the water. They crept forward, forming a circle behind Kellan and Kieran, the two remaining Princes in the Seelie Court. Once, there had been many Princes and Princesses… before Maeve had killed them all, sneaky and power hungry as she was. Princesses poisoned by mysterious corsets given as presents. Princes found dead, stabbed in the throes of passion with some unknown seductress. Children taken into forests for a pleasant picnic and somehow *lost*, never to return…

One by one, Maeve charmed and betrayed them all. Even her own sister and brother in law, Kellan's parents, had fallen under her spell and paid the price. No one could resist the Queen, no one but Kellan and Kieran.

So here they were, ready to fight to the death. To avenge their parents, their brothers and sisters, their cousins. All the deaths that Maeve had caused would come back to her tenfold. Tonight, or a thousand years from now, it did not matter. That was the way of things.

Finally, Maeve took a breath.

"Do you know, when you were born, we wondered which of you would be the Light and which the Dark," she said, almost as if musing aloud. Of course, at the same time she projected her melodic voice, making sure her followers in the Court could hear every word. "We didn't know a thing until you each used your magic for the first time, which took years."

Kellan merely arched a brow, his fingers itching to draw his sword and run her through. End this all, right here and now. Maeve's lips curled up, as if she knew his thoughts perfectly, and they merely amused her.

"That lovely white magic you have, Prince of Light. Bringing life to everything you touch, making things grow and thrive, making them pure…" she said to Kellan before turning her gaze to Kieran. "And then there is you, our Dark Prince. If I hadn't seen your birth, I wouldn't believe you to be Kellan's flesh and blood. Your magic is dark as night, freezing everything it touches. I remember the first time you saw a pretty bird in the sky, you raised your hand to point it out to your brother. It dropped from the sky like a stone, falling dead at your feet."

She chuckled at the angry flush that lit Kieran's ruddy cheeks before continuing.

"I tried to get my sister to drown you that day, did you

know? I told her to kill you, or take you out in the world and exchange you for a lovely human boy. You're a wild one, maybe you could have survived as a Changeling," she said, cocking her head and narrowing her gaze. "Too late for that now, I suppose. So what shall I do with you, Prince of Shadows?"

Kellan reached out a hand to his brother, trying to stop the response he knew was coming, but it was too late. Kieran's notorious temper flared bright, threatening to burn them both to ash.

"What will you do with us?" Kieran growled, drawing his sword. The sound of the sword leaving the scabbard rang in the air, the finality of it sending a chill across Kellan's skin. "I think you are asking the wrong questions, my Queen. Perhaps you should ask what we will do with you. You murdered our parents in their sleep, throats slit in their own bed. There is a cost to be paid for that, dear Aunt."

Maeve's amused smile spread into a deadly grin.

"And you imagine yourself the one who will extract that price, nephew? How terribly *exciting* for us all."

"You cannot think to kill the last of your family line, my Queen," Kellan broke in.

Her brows arched in surprise.

"I would do no such thing," she protested, giving a beat's pause. "You will still be quite alive, Kellan. With the Prince of Light as my consort, my heirs will be many. The royal Seelie bloodline will multiply, with a quickness."

The last was said with a teasing, flirtatious wink that made Kellan's stomach flip-flop.

"Never. I will never lay with you, Aunt. Nor will I allow you to take my brother from me," he said, glancing at Kieran, who now glared at Kellan in turn. As if Kellan had brought this about, somehow.

"You think to defy me?" Maeve hissed, rising from her

chair, dagger in her fist. "What will a pair of lads do against the strength of the Summer court?"

She gestured, raising her hands to beckon her supporters, who drew closer with a collective *hiss*. There were many who envied the royal family, who thought themselves a better match for the Queen's consort and confidante. *Let them have it*, Kellan thought. Could they not see that this was the Queen's true nature, that they would only be in the same position in the not-terribly-distant future?

"Last chance," the Queen taunted, waving her dagger at Kellan. "If you strike the blow, take the Shadow Prince's life, take his power to combine with your own, you can have everything you've ever wanted. Never again will anyone mistake you for him. You will rise as Queen's consort, rule the Faerie realms by my side. Your children will have power beyond imagining…"

Kellan faltered for a moment, trying to imagine a world without his twin. Where he alone rose to be powerful, respected, beloved. Where his trickster brother never stole another woman from his bed, never made him feel guilty for being more loved and admired than Kieran, less feared. That moment's pause drew a growl from Kieran, who launched himself toward the Queen, sword raised high.

The Queen raised a hand, smacking Kieran down with an invisible wall of magic, as easily and casually as she might swat at an insect buzzing about her head. Kieran crumpled, his sword tumbling to the side as he collapsed. He fell in place, and didn't move again.

"Kieran," Kellan whispered under his breath, looking wildly between the Queen and his twin.

"Do it!" the Queen urged, thinking Kellan was tempted to attack his brother. Her smile was so wide that Kellan could see every tooth in her mouth, all sharp, gleaming, and *eager*.

He took a step toward Kieran, slipping his hand into his

pocket and produced a dagger much like the wicked blade the Queen held.

"Yes," she hissed. "Only the Light Prince may kill the Dark, tip the scales of the Faerie realm. Finish what I have started, my Prince, and we can be together for eternity. Imagine…"

Kellan dropped to his knees to shield his brother, flinging the dagger straight at the Queen. It missed her heart by inches, burrowing into the flesh below her shoulder and drawing a long, high scream from her lips.

"Traitor!" she screamed, power flooding her voice. Kellan knew that if her words were true, she couldn't kill them… but she could banish them to another plane. Power gathered and shimmered around her as her face contorted with rage, and he knew her next words before she screamed them. "You. Are. BANISHED!"

Gripping Kieran around the waist, Kellan closed his eyes and gritted his teeth as the spell ripped him away from the fabric of the Faerie realm. The monarch's word was law, and in Faerie that meant the whole world bent to her will. Her words became reality the moment she spoke them…

A flash of light, and then Kellan and Kieran were dumped in a broad, grassy moor of sorts. Miles and miles and miles of nothing but heather and grass. Not a house or a person or even a tree to be seen. Kellan couldn't be sure, but he had the idea that the Faerie Queen had favored them a bit by dumping him here in the human realm and not one of a hundred other exceedingly unpleasant planes of existence.

Still, it was something of a shock. For the first time in their royal lives, Kellan and Kieran were truly *alone*. As interesting as that was, this was hardly the time to wax philosophical about their situation. Kieran needed healing, and from the looks of this place, any food or medicine worth having was a long, long way away.

Picking his brother up with a grunt, Kellan tossed Kieran over his shoulder and began to walk north.

Toward what, he had no idea...

New Orleans, Louisiana
Present Day

"I should have left you to Maeve, you backstabbing son of a goat," Kellan drawled, casting Kieran a scowl as they strode through the Marginy on their way to the Manor. His Irish accent always thickened when he was irritable or excited, and just now it would be nearly incomprehensible to a passing stranger.

"You're honestly that upset? She's just a girl," Kieran said, huffing a laugh. His twin could be downright melodramatic at times. "Not terribly loyal, either. Really, I did you a favor."

"A favor, is it now?" Kellan growled. "You fucked the girl I've been seeing for the past three months. According to her, you didn't say a word, and she didn't know you weren't me."

Kieran rolled his eyes.

"Liar. She knew we weren't the same person, she just wanted to walk on the wild side. No matter how far we get from the Court, people just seem to know. Just like the ones I try to date always gravitate to you, blathering about the goodness in you and all that nonsense. It goes both ways, eh?"

Kellan's lack of response was enough for Kieran. His brother would get over it soon enough.

"At least she wasn't your fated woman," Kieran said, clapping Kellan on the shoulder as the Manor came into view. "Who you'll never meet if we're late to this meeting. Rhys runs a very timely program, here."

It was true. Kieran and Kellan had spent over a thousand years rollicking and rolling, narrowly escaping danger, and generally doing anything they wanted — all over the wide human world, and a few other planes. Every century or so they'd have a terrible fight, then spin off in their own directions, having adventures on their own. Always, though, they gravitated back toward one another.

Two halves of a whole, as their mother used to tell them. It might be true enough, but that didn't make the concept any less tiresome.

Now that they'd been recruited as members of the Alpha Guardians, or *rescued* as Rhys Macaulay referred to their abduction and brief imprisonment *for the good of the city*... now, they had to live by *rules*. The Gray brothers, as they'd taken to calling themselves, didn't really follow rules very well.

"Rhys and the lads are already outside," Kellan said, nodding toward the Guardians gathered on the front steps of the Manor.

"Waiting for us, I suppose," Kieran grumbled. "Not like we just did twelve hours of patrol or anything..."

"We did sign up for this," Kellan said with a shrug. "Did the ceremony and all."

"The only other option was to let them imprison us at the Manor until they felt the big bad threat over New Orleans had subsided. Not much of a choice, that."

They strode up the front lawn and joined the circle where Rhys, Gabriel, Aeric, and Asher stood discussing the state of affairs.

"What'd we miss?" Kieran said, by way of greeting.

"Took you long enough to get here," Gabriel groused.

"Alright, alright," Kellan said, waving him down. "Just

because Cassie's due any day now and you're a bundle of nerves doesn't mean you should jump all over us. We were dispatching a bunch of Trillah demons in the Central Business District. Ease off."

"We were talking about Pere Mal's disappearance," Asher said, always the sober voice of reason. The man was so stoic he was practically a robot, which was funny compared to Kira, his little spitfire of a mate. "We haven't heard a single thing from his camp in weeks now. He's just *gone*."

"Yet every single one of his minions seems busier than ever," Aeric pointed out.

"Yeah, but when we corner one of the buggers they seem different. They used to be kind of gleeful in their evildoing now they just seem... terrified," Gabriel concluded.

"Echo's hearing whispers about a new guy running the show. Similar name to Pere Mal, even, but... no one will talk. Her usual sources are all running scared, keeping themselves out of the limelight. I tried to run down Ciprian the Vampyre a couple days ago, and even he looked nervous."

"That's saying something," Aeric said with a frown. "Ciprian is one of the cockiest people I've ever encountered. I use the term *people* liberally."

"I still think this comes back to Cassie's prediction about Kieran and Kellan," Gabriel said, crossing his arms. "She prophesied that if Pere Mal didn't kill them, someone bigger and more dangerous would come looking for them."

"Not us," Kieran interrupted. "Don't lay this at our feet. The big bad wolf is supposed to be hunting a fated mate. One of us is supposed to fall for a girl, and she'll be the target, not us."

"Yeah, but if the new boss is anything like Pere Mal, he'll be hunting you to find her," Gabriel said.

"This is all pointless anyway, since neither of us has been

love-struck," Kellan said, then arched a brow at Kieran. "Unless you've caught feelings for Emma?"

Kieran squinted.

"Who?" he asked. His twin's scowl made it clear that Emma was the girl Kieran had scooped from Kellan only the night before. "Ah, yeah, no fears on that front."

"Apparently not," Kellan snapped.

"Well, with all the fuss, I think this makes it clear that you're the one who's going to end up with the doomed damsel in distress as your fated mate," Kieran said, unable to resist digging the knife in a little deeper.

Kellan's cheeks flushed with anger, but he didn't get another word in.

"Sorry to interrupt this charming discussion," Asher said, "But we have bigger things to worry about. Pere Mal and the new guy might be working behind the scenes, but we still have other tasks to complete. Namely, there's a pretty aggressive nest of young Vampyres in the Treme, and they're proving to be unpleasant neighbors."

"They snatched and bit a kid last night," Rhys sighed. "And this is after a number of other complaints. We have to clear out the whole nest and burn the house to the ground, make sure they don't come back. You know how territorial Vampyres can be."

"What are we waiting for, then?" Kieran said. "Let's go raze 'em to the ground."

Shaking his head, Kieran followed the rest of the Guardians to the waiting SUV, ready to do some damage.

"Hell," Kieran said, shaking a clump of bloody goo off his sword hand. "Have I mentioned that Vampyres are *disgusting*? Not to mention their taste in interior decor. This whole house is stuck halfway between an opium den and something out of an Anne Rice novel. It's very imaginative, is it?"

"Aye, but at least the job's done," Rhys said, surveying the room with little humor. "It looks like we've got them all, don't you think?"

Gabriel stalked across the room with a grimace, pausing to wipe his blade on a velvet curtain.

"This nest makes my skin crawl," Gabriel griped. "Just in time, here comes the upstairs contingent."

Aeric came down the rickety stairs first, then Asher appeared, supporting Kellan as he walked with an obvious limp.

"What the fuck's wrong with you, then?" Kieran said. His words were cavalier, but it didn't stop him from hurrying across the room to check on his brother.

"Damned Vampyre bit me on the leg!" Kellan groaned. "On the *leg*, for Chrissakes. I've never taken so much pleasure in decapitation before, I swear it."

"Did he manage to get his poison in you?" Rhys asked, following Kieran over to examine Kellan's injury. "Och, yeah, the skin around the bite's already turning dark. We'll have to get you to the emergency room, I think."

Kellan's expression darkened. "I hate the hospital."

Kieran signaled to Aeric, taking over as the support post for his brother.

"Don't be a child," Kieran prodded his brother. True to form, Kellan snapped to his own defense.

"Anyone who got trapped and vivisected by the London Royal Society would hate doctors. It was a month before you noticed they were holding me!" he protested.

"It was the early 1600s, there was barely a mail service those days. Besides, it's been four centuries. Don't you think it's time to conquer your fears, little brother?"

"Little brother, my ass," Kellan muttered as Kieran helped him outside and into the back seat of the Guardians' SUV. "Mother never told us who was born first, you just think you're superior. Mostly because you're delusional."

Aeric and Rhys climbed in the front, and Aeric drove toward the Gray Market.

"Consider the evidence," Kieran said, keeping up the banter between them. No doubt, Kellan's wound was already growing painful; a distraction wouldn't hurt. He ticked off thoughts on his fingers. "I'm a Prince of the Summer Court. I can use glamour to change my shape. I've learned to genuinely shapeshift, and my bear is gorgeous. I can wield strong elemental magic, I can jump between most of the planes of existence without effort—"

"We're twins, you horse's ass," Kellan said with a roll of his eyes.

"I'm just stating facts here, no need to get touchy. Or is this the old Light versus Dark debate? Are you still sore about being what is clearly the lesser of two great powers?" Kieran cocked a brow in a challenging way, knowing it would rile Kellan further.

"Will you two shut the hell up?" Aeric said as he pulled up in front of an abandoned house just north of the French Quarter. "It's like driving around with two children in the back seat."

"Is this the new portal to Sloane General?" Kieran asked, peering at the ivy-covered, hole-riddled house. For the sake of expediency the hospital had its own private entrance, separate from the rest of the Gray Market. "Last I saw, it was all the way down in the Holy Cross neighborhood."

"As it happens, the Guardians have their own entrance to Sloane. Several of them, actually, sprinkled around the city. We seem to need the emergency services more than your average bear shifter," Rhys explained.

"Posh," Kellan jested. A glance at him revealed that he was beginning to sweat a little. It took a lot to make one of the Gray brothers show discomfort, so Kieran climbed out of the car and dragged Kellan out too.

"Alright, I think there's an opportunity here," Kieran told him as he and Rhys helped get Kellan up the house's cinderblock front steps. They stepped through the bolt-hole, feeling the brief loss of gravity, and then walked right into a familiar corridor. They were no more than a hundred yards from the ER's admitting desk now.

"What's that?" Kellan asked, his jaw tight with the obvious effort of suppressing his pain.

"There are tons of hot Kith nurses at this place. You could use a little nurturing, brother. And probably to get laid—"

"Hey, hi," Aeric called to the triage nurse who peered up from the admitting desk. "Alpha Guardians. This one's got a nasty vamp bite, big dose of poison. Gonna need to see a doc, ASAP."

"Oh!" the petite blonde nurse said, jumping up. "Come over to the first exam room, okay?"

She led them into a small room with an examination table and two chairs. Turning to the Guardians, she pursed her lips.

"Can you get Dr. Khouri for us, if she's here? We've worked with her several times," Aeric asked the nurse.

"Dr. Khouri is always here," the nurse said with a little smirk. "I'll be sure to get her for you."

She settled Kellan on the exam table.

"Try to relax," she told him. "Have you seen Dr. Khouri before?"

"No, she sees some of the Guardians' mates," Kieran cut in.

"I see. Well I'll go grab her now. Only one of y'all can stay in here with him, though," she told them with an apologetic frown. "The other two need to give us a little room to work."

Aeric and Rhys left the room without a question, taking seats just outside the room. They could still see through the glass if they turned around, so it wasn't much of a sacrifice. Left to their own devices, Kieran and Kellan shared a look.

Kellan opened his mouth, about to start talking smack. Then he froze, brow furrowing. Kieran turned, wondering what could possibly have shut his twin down so fast.

Outside the room stood a gorgeous woman in a white doctor's coat. She was petite but curvy, her sexy figure apparent even through her scrubs and lab coat. She had creamy caramel skin and a long curtain of raven's-wing hair. Clutching a stack of patient charts, she didn't so much as glance up as she made her way toward Kieran and Kellan.

Kieran's heart and gut lurched as one, the force of the feeling almost brought him to his knees.

Mine! his soul cried.

And then, a moment later, *mate*.

His heart pounded in his chest, his hands shaking, the need to touch her almost unbearable. It was happening, just like Cassie predicted. Kieran had doubted her before, but now it was so, so clear.

"I found my—" he started to say, then stopped and snapped his gaze to his brother. Kellan had been speaking, and damn if it didn't sound like he'd just said…

"Fated mate," Kellan finished.

Kieran could feel himself gaping at his brother like an idiot, saw the same dumbstruck expression on his twin's face.

"Oh *hell* no," Kieran hissed, baring his teeth.

Kellan could have anything else in this world, anything. Kieran would lay down his life for Kellan without a thought.

But this girl… this woman… she was *his*.

CHAPTER 1

I have got to be one of the unluckiest people on the planet, she thought. *Plain and simple.*

Dr. Serafina Khouri bit her lip as she juggled what felt like a mile-high stack of patient charts.

Okay, okay. My life isn't that bad. I have a job, I have a home. I shouldn't be so whiny. But still...

So far, this Tuesday morning shift at Sloane General's emergency services department wasn't really treating her too well. After arriving at four forty five in the morning, fifteen minutes before her shift was supposed to start, she waded into a seemingly endless line of cases.

A fire at a popular Vampyre club had filled the ER with Kith patients complaining of minor burns and smoke inhalation. A fight had broken out amongst a bunch of wolf shifters at a Motorcycle Club rally, which meant Sera was treating broken noses, vicious bite marks, and a couple of concussions. In the middle of all that, a Bejahhb demon had gone into labor in the waiting room, and the birth of six squirming and tentacled baby demons had nearly wiped Sera out.

Sera herself had dropped two trays of surgical instruments, ripped the seat out of her scrub pants, and burned the sensitive skin of her inner arm on the Bejahhb mother's acidic afterbirth. All of that was in the first six hours of her shift, too. She dragged herself through the rest of her shift with blessedly few incidents. Well, no more incidents with *patients*.

The staff were a different matter. Though Sera had worked at Sloane General just over a year, she wasn't terribly popular amongst some of the staff. Specifically, Dr. Gregor Day and all the nurses and doctors who hung on his every word. The handsome French gargoyle had targeted Sera from her first day at Sloane, asking her out on a date within minutes of meeting her.

Date wasn't even the right word for what he'd proposed. He'd asked her if she wanted to come over to his apartment for a bottle of wine, "and maybe a movie… if we get that far". With an accompanying wiggle of eyebrows, implying that they would be too busy having energetic sex to watch a movie.

Sera had flushed and turned him down, offended by his amorous presumption. Unbeknownst to Sera, she'd set herself on a particularly difficult path for the rest of her employment at Sloane General.

Her rejection of Dr. Day's advances had seemed a shock to Gregor, and made a good bit of gossip for the hospital staff. Like how *dare* Sera turn down the tall, dark, and handsome doctor that everyone secretly longed for? Not only did Sera have a strict policy against dating coworkers, but she also found Gregor to be pushy and egotistical.

Besides, Dr. Day had a distinctly unfair advantage over Sera, though it took her a while to discover the fact. Gargoyles had a ton of natural healing magic flowing in their veins, which meant Gregor could just waltz in and fix nearly any ailment. The ease of his work made Sera green with envy.

Her adoptive parents were a hedge witch and a falcon shifter, but Sera's own Kith powers remained a mystery. Every once in a while she could fire off a little healing magic, but for the most part she had to work her butt off to care for her patients. Her own stubbornness was the only thing that had propelled Sera this far into her medical career, that and a lot of late nights. She'd be damned if she was going to let one man's big ego foil all she'd worked for.

She sighed as she left a patient's room, feeling restless even though she hadn't stopped moving all morning. She always felt this way just after a full moon, like she was missing something... but what? The corners of her mouth tugged downward as she thought of the way she lost herself during the full moon, whole hours that disappeared...

Better not to think of that. Waking up sore and forgetful didn't mean she was doing something bad. Just... mysterious, even to herself. Between that and the dreams, those vivid dreams about whole lives she'd never lived, people she'd loved and lost and yet never even known...

Yeah, Sera had a lot going on in her life right now.

"Dr. Khouri."

Sera turned to find Dr. Adeem, the Chief of Medicine, standing behind her with an impatient expression.

"Dr. Adeem, good morning. Or afternoon?" Sera corrected herself, frowning at her wristwatch.

"It is nearly six in the evening, Dr. Khouri," Dr. Adeem said in his crisp Pakistani accent, looking down at Sera over the bridge of his glasses. "Are you feeling quite all right?"

"Yes, of course," Sera blurted out. "Just a busy day. Like every day, ha ha."

An awkward moment passed, Dr. Adeem narrowing his gaze at Sera.

"Fine," he said at last. "I know your shift is nearly done, but I'd like you to see one last patient. One of the Alpha Guardians has come in with a Vampyre bite. Since we consider them VIPs, I would like you to see them before you leave."

"Me?" Sera asked, embarrassed at how surprised she sounded.

Dr. Adeem's frown deepened.

"Yes, you. Dr. Khouri, I know you've had a little trouble adjusting to Sloane General, but you are an excellent doctor. Very thorough and knowledgeable. I know you will give the patient the best care possible."

He lifted his brows, as if challenging her to question his statement.

"Thank you," Sera said, blushing. "I— I'll go see him now."

Before she could ruin the moment, she whirled and started down the hallway.

"Dr. Khouri!" Dr. Adeem called, pointing down the hallway. "They're in Exam Room One. The other way."

She halted and wheeled around with a grimace, giving him a quick wave and an awkward chuckle as she headed the other direction.

Smooth, Sera.

She wanted to get out of Dr. Adeem's sightline so badly that she had to keep herself from breaking into a sprint as she headed for the ER. She nearly lost her stack of charts in her enthusiasm, and was still wrestling them as she approached the door of the exam room.

Frowning, she plucked her new patient's chart from the doorway and flipped it open. Usually she liked to give it a brief read-over before she consulted with the patient, which meant that by the time she introduced herself she already had a fair idea of the patient's complaints and which questions needed to be asked.

"Kellan Gray?" she asked at last, stepping fully into the room.

She glanced up and did a double take. There were two of them, two huge hulking men with silvery-brown hair, impossibly broad shoulders, chiseled jaws, and piercing green eyes.

Twins. Holy *crap*.

"Aye," the one seated on the exam table said.

There was something, some subtext between the two men, all in a brief glance. Sera opened her mouth to speak, but suddenly she felt strange. Hot, burning hot. But freezing cold, too. Like her skin was ice, but some strange heat was bubbling up from inside her, lava rising under a dormant volcano, ready to blow the top off it all.

Looking at them gave her the oddest sensation, almost… possessive? Like a voice whispering *mine*. Before she could think too much on that, she broke into a heavy sweat all over her body.

"Dr. Khouri?" one of the men said, reaching out to her.

Then Sera felt her whole body shudder. Saw a brilliant white wave of magic burst free from her body, even as her eyes rolled up in her head.

She didn't feel herself hit the floor, but she went down, down, down…

CHAPTER 2

Kellan and Kieran lunged for her at the same time. Kellan growled low in his throat when his knee went out under him, meaning that Kieran swooped in and grabbed the girl before she could hit the ground. Just watching Kieran catch her and cradle her in his arms, staring down at the pretty doctor with something close to awe…

It *hurt*. More than his damn leg, deeper.

"A little help, here!" Kieran shouted.

"You fucking bastard," Kellan growled.

Several nurses rushed in and pulled Dr. Khouri from Kieran's arms, leaving Kieran free to turn on Kellan instead.

"She's mine," Kieran snarled.

"Like hell," Kellan swore.

Kieran surprised him by shifting into his bear form, something they usually only did to fit in with the other Guardians. Heedless of his wound, Kellan shifted with a roar, the pain in his leg giving him a slight advantage.

Fuck no, he wasn't going to let his scheming asshole of a brother *near* his mate. Kellan went straight for Kieran's throat, and all the other Kith made themselves scarce as the brothers engaged in a vicious, furious fight.

They would have continued like that, a violent whirl of fur and destruction, if Rhys hadn't stepped back into the room and put his fingers to his lips to release a heart-stoppingly loud whistle.

Kellan faltered first, enough for Kieran to swipe sharp claws across his shoulder. Kellan released a bellow of pain, his rage rising again.

"ENOUGH!" Rhys thundered.

That got their attention.

"Shift, right now," Rhys hissed, looking like he murder them both on the spot. "This is unacceptable. We are Alpha Guardians, not lads in a public pissing contest."

Kieran shifted first, and Kellan begrudgingly followed him.

"You, sit the fuck down and don't move until your leg has been treated," Rhys told Kellan. Then he turned to Kieran.

"You, go wash the blood off your knuckles and check on the doctor. I don't want to see either of you so much as looking at the other until you've cooled off."

Kieran vanished with a scowl, Rhys right behind him. A particularly pushy older male nurse forced Kellan to sit down again, unconcerned at the way Kellan growled and gripped the table with white knuckles.

Kieran vanished for a long time, presumably attending Dr. Khouri into another room, only to reappear halfway through the excruciating treatment of Kellan's Vampyre bite. Kellan glared at his twin, who glared right back at him. Both their arms were crossed, jaws set in the same stubborn line.

Yeah, this was going to get nasty, fast.

"What's happening with the doctor?" Kellan asked.

"Serafina," Kieran informed him with a superior little grin. "Sera for short."

Kellan muttered a curse, but he didn't want to tick off the nurse cleaning out his wound with the lightest of touches. He needed to be fit for action, stat.

"And?" he prompted.

"They're not sure why she fainted," Kieran said with a half shrug. "Aeric and one of the doctors are with her, trying to figure it out."

"Seemed like a big burst of power, out of nowhere."

Kieran nodded noncommittally. Before they could continue their half-conversation, Rhys burst into the room, pointing a finger at Kieran.

"Is it true?" he asked, his Scottish burr deep and thick.

"What?" Kieran asked.

"Is she the mate? Your mate, I mean?" he asked.

Kieran shot Kellan a look.

"She is."

"Like hell," Kellan popped off.

Rhys turned to Kellan.

"What does that mean?"

"We both got the same sensation from her, the mating call." Kellan arched a brow. "And I'm not letting him take this one from me. She's *mine*."

"Over my dead fucking body," Kieran snarled.

The nurse tending Kellan's leg tied off the gauze dressing and stood up.

"You're good to go, but you need to take it easy," the man said, giving Kellan a stern look.

"Bad time to be on bed rest," Kieran taunted.

Kellan stepped toward him with a growl rumbling in his chest, but Rhys stopped him with a hand.

"We have bigger things to worry about here, boys. We need to take the doctor back to the Manor and keep her under lock and key until we figure out how she fits into the prophecy." He paused, looking between them. "Can you two be civil for long enough to get her in the car? I'll need to talk to the hospital administrators, let them know she's going to need a few days of leave."

"Yes," they replied as one, then shot each other a furious look.

Rhys gave them one final look of warning, then turned and strode from the room.

"Let's just get through this, okay?" Kellan said.

Kieran was already out the door, leaving Kellan to trail in his wake. Typical.

Kellan let Kieran take charge, unwilling to start a battle over who was more alpha when his unconscious, prone mate was in the middle of it. After getting an all-clear from the doctors, who'd roused her briefly and discharged her, the twins got her out to the parking lot.

As if by magic, the Guardians' butler Duverjay was waiting just outside in one of their SUVs, engine idling. Rhys had been quite busy, it seemed.

"Rhys and Aeric will be driving the other vehicle back," Duverjay informed them once Kieran and Sera had settled in the back seat, Kellan in the front. "The Manor is aflutter with anticipation for her arrival."

Settling which room she'd be assigned in the Manor, no doubt. Kellan's hands bunched into fists once more, a burst of stubborn pride flaring in his chest. This was no time for a fistfight, certainly, but he couldn't be so passive as to let his twin sweep the girl off her feet.

Not. Happening.

But how to find the balance?

Luckily, their arrival at the Manor was relatively smooth. Mere Marie swept in and took charge, putting the doctor… Sera, he reminded himself, in a guest room with two empty bedrooms on either side. Without even glancing at Kieran, Kellan knew they'd both be moving their meager possessions into those rooms later in the evening.

If Kieran's desire to be close to Sera was anything like his own, it must be killing him. Not that Kieran ever felt deeply for any woman he took into his bed, of course. Kellan was pretty certain that he held deeper and truer feelings than his brother ever would.

"I expect you two downstairs within twenty minutes," Mere Marie told them crisply once Sera was ensconced in the guest room. "I'm keeping the chaos at bay for the moment, but there's a lot to discuss. We're having a group meeting as soon as you two present yourselves."

"We don't know any more than you do," Kellan said, but she just held up a hand.

"Twenty minutes," she repeated, then left the room in a rustle of robes. "And don't scare her off. Rhys told me you two are already fighting over the poor thing."

Kellan rolled his eyes. Alright, maybe he and Kieran had gotten into their share of childish fights over minor things here and there. And maybe they weren't even a bit ashamed of it. All the Guardians had seen of the Gray twins was arguably not their *best*.

"Aye-aye, Captain," Kieran said, snapping her a salute even though she'd already left.

"Nice comeback," Kellan said.

Kieran opened his mouth, but Sera herself interrupted, stirring under the comforter.

"Where am I? Oh god, did I faint?" she asked, wrinkling her nose. Her accent was American with the faintest undertone of something exotic, enchanting.

Kellan's words stuck in his throat for a second. He was far too busy looking into the depths of Sera's big brown eyes, precisely the color of melted chocolate. Framed by dark lashes, set above a proud nose and a lush mouth, they were stunning beyond words.

"I'm Kieran, and this is Kellan. You're safe. We're Guardians, and we brought you back to our house," Kieran jumped in.

"What? Why?" she asked. Her puzzled frown was more cute than concerning, tugging at the tight knot of nerves in Kellan's chest. "Wait… why… do I know you? You both look so familiar to me…"

Kellan glanced at Kieran, then reached out to pat Sera's hand. She surprised him by turning her hand over, slipping it into his, giving his hand a soft squeeze. In another circumstance it would have been a gesture of comfort, but just now it seemed full of worried questions and doubt. Just as quickly, she released him, pulling her hand back and tucking it close to her body. As if his touch had burned her delicate skin somehow.

"I don't think so, but… that might be the mating pull," Kellan said, trying to keep his tone gentle.

"The *what*?!" she yelped, fingers clutching at the covers.

"Listen, don't worry about that right now," Kieran said.

"You're safe and sound, and we'll work out the rest later."

"Why did you bring me here?" she asked, reaching up to touch the back of her head.

Another glance between the twins.

"You were cleared by the doctors at Sloane," Kellan assured her. "But you should rest. You fired off a huge burst of energy, which can be very draining. We can talk about the rest of it tomorrow, when you're recharged."

Sera opened her mouth, then seemed to think better of it.

"This is your house?" she asked, a skeptical look in her eyes.

"Shared by all the Guardians," Kellan said. "There's a buzzer here by your bedside, so you can ring for the butler if you need anything at all. We'll take good care of you, Dr. Khouri."

"Sera," she said, then flushed at her automatic response. "Just Sera, if you please."

"Sera," Kellan repeated, loving the feel of it on his tongue as he said it. "We will talk more tomorrow, I promise."

She looked between them once more, the blush on her cheeks growing darker, but she only nodded. When she didn't speak again, Kellan and Kieran rose and left the room. Kieran's expression was unreadable as they headed downstairs in perfect silence, each caught up in their own thoughts.

The skin of Kellan's palm still tingled where Sera had touched him. It was embarrassing, but that simple touch had set him afire, made his body tighten and ache.

Damn, this was going to get ugly, and fast.

Still, Kellan knew himself, knew his heart. He more than wanted Sera, he needed her. She called out to him, without him even knowing the most basic parts of her personality. He'd always heard this about fated mates, but now that it was happening to him…

He wouldn't let her go, not while he still lived and breathed.

Never.

CHAPTER 3

*S*era frowned down at herself, then glanced up into the oversized mirror in the guest bathroom. When she woke, she found several pretty and colorful dresses in her size hanging on the back of the bedroom door. There were also two pairs of shoes, giving her a choice between heels and flats.

She'd nudged the heels away with her bare foot, slipping into the flats. Her first frown was because they'd fit perfectly. Who the hell had found shoes for her in the middle of the night, while she'd been sleeping?

The second frown was directed at her reflection, her body encased in a stunning lavender dress complete with lacy frills that hid every potential flaw. This dress made her look *amazing*. But... where had it come from?

Clearly the person that picked it out was considering her size and shape, but didn't know that Sera hardly ever wore dresses or overtly feminine clothes. She liked tailored slacks and elegant silk shirts, maybe with a vest for flair. And she nearly always wore clean Converse or her chunky work shoes, made for comfort over style.

Still… she couldn't complain. She couldn't recognize the name of the designer scrawled on the tag, but this dress was almost definitely French and super fancy. Plus, considering the two shockingly handsome men who'd been staring at her like she was the last woman on the whole planet, she could afford to look a little girly today.

She wandered out of her room and headed downstairs, following the sound of feminine laughter that echoed through the house. She found a huge open room downstairs, with a lounge and kitchen and meeting area. All the Guardians were conspicuously absent, but five women sat around a big table sipping coffee. A man in a formal tuxedo, presumably the butler Kellan had mentioned, hovered nearby as if waiting to be beckoned.

"Ah! Dr. Khouri!" A graceful older woman with coffee-and-cream skin and flowing robes stood and waved her over. "Come meet the ladies."

"Hi," Sera said. "It's just Sera, please. Um…"

She cast a glance around. The woman gave her a knowing smile that made Sera's stomach flutter.

"Kieran and Kellan are out on a mission with the other Guardians. They'll be back shortly," she said, flapping a dismissive hand. "Sit, sit. I'm Mere Marie, something of… you could say, the den mother?"

One of the women smothered something that sounded like a huff of laughter, but didn't say anything. Sera took an unoccupied seat as she was introduced to the stunning women mated to the other Guardians. *Kira, Echo, Cassie, and Alice*, Sera repeated to herself half a dozen times in an effort to remember them all. Cassie was the easiest, because she was immensely pregnant and grinning like a fool.

"Would you like some breakfast? Duverjay was going to serve some omelettes and croissants and cafe au lait, I believe," Mere Marie asked.

"I'm famished, actually," Sera admitted with a smile. "My schedule's completely wrecked now, I think."

"Welcome to the Manor," Kira said, smiling over her coffee cup. "You'll get used to it."

There was a moment of silence, then Kira blushed.

"Was I not supposed to say that? Y'all told me almost the same thing when Asher dragged me in here the first time!" she protested.

The women chuckled, but Mere Marie shook her head.

"Sera, I'm afraid we don't quite know what to make of you," she said slowly. "We are fairly certain that you feature in certain... prophecies... and that you're in grave danger."

"Me?" Sera asked, accepting a cup of milky coffee from the butler. "Thanks."

"Duverjay, ma'am," he said with the briefest of bows, then whisked off to the kitchen and proceeded to work on cooking something that smelled absolutely amazing.

"Sera," Cassie said, reaching out across the table to get Sera's attention. "I'm an Oracle, so I get a lot of visions and premonitions. I've never seen *you*, exactly, but I have witnessed a lot of prophecies that involve Kieran and Kellan."

Sera gave her a blank look.

"And their mate," Cassie added, pulling an uncertain expression.

"I don't understand," Sera said point-blank.

"Well... we're pretty sure you're Kieran's fated mate," Echo jumped in. "Or Kellan? We're not sure. We were hoping you could tell us, actually."

Sera sucked in a breath and picked up her coffee, sipping it for a moment of reprieve.

"Which one of them do you feel sort of... pulled toward?" Mere Marie asked.

"Um. Both of them? It's kind of equal," Sera said, feeling her face heat.

"Oooh," Alice said, leaning in on her elbows. "A menage mateship. Imagine that!"

Just as Sera was about to die with shame, Kira patted her elbow.

"Some things are just meant to be," the other woman said with a shrug. "I'd hate to be the one who has to listen to them argue forever, but I wouldn't mind sleeping between those two at night."

Sera couldn't help but laugh, and her tension eased a little. Was Alice right? Was Sera meant to be with two men, forever? Or was she just being offered a choice, Kieran or Kellan?

"They were fighting over you the whole time you slept," Echo informed her.

"Oh," was all Sera could manage, then a sigh. "This is so overwhelming."

Everyone chuckled. Duverjay started delivering plates of fluffy omelettes and buttery croissants, and for a minute everyone was absorbed in the food. After a bit, the conversation picked up again.

"It's always like that with taking a Guardian as your mate," Cassie confided. "We've all run into the same things. They're big bullies who need to dominate and protect. You just have to draw the line, and stick to your guns."

"I don't mean to be rude," Kira said, "but what *are* you? I've been trying to read you since you walked in, and it's making me nuts."

"Me? Nothing, really. I'm Kith, but I'm basically powerless," Sera replied.

There was a beat of silence.

"What?" she asked.

"It's just, the Guardians usually attract these really insanely powerful mates. Women with so much power that they need to be protected from the big bad world outside," Cassie joked, rolling her eyes.

Sera bit her lip, wrinkling her nose.

"I don't know what to tell you. I'm adopted, and my parents know I'm not a shifter or a witch like either of them, so…" She ended with a lift of her shoulders. "Maybe this is a mistake, like wires crossed?"

"Hah!" Mere Marie crowed. "Not likely. You're something, alright. And Kieran and Kellan aren't just confused. You're a true match for them, I promise you. Not just a doctor."

"If you say so," Sera said, her stomach churning. She pushed her plate away, appetite vanished.

"If you don't mind, Sera, I'd like for you to let Cassie hold your hand for a few moments. Maybe she can get some kind of reading off you?" Mere Marie lifted her brows.

"Of course."

Sera held out her hand, and Cassie grasped her wrist. Half a moment later Cassie ripped her hand away from Sera, sputtering. The pretty redhead turned her head away, retching quietly and pushing back from the table.

"Are you okay?" Echo said, jumping up. Everyone stood and fussed over Cassie, who was dry heaving and wiping tears from her face.

Sera sat perfectly still, uncomprehending and ashamed at once. What the heck had she done? In the midst of the confusion, the Guardians returned, flooding the room with concerned and jittery men.

Cassie's mate Gabriel, who Sera had previously met at Sloane General, wrapped her up in his arms and did his best to soothe her. All the other women gravitated to their mates, too. After a moment Sera realized that Kieran and Kellan were standing just behind her, their expressions stormy.

"Was there a prophecy?" Kellan asked. "Tell us!"

"She needs rest," Gabriel snapped.

"No, I just… Oh!" Cassie managed after a moment. "Oh, god. I… I saw you die, Sera. I saw you ripped apart!"

She burst into tears, and Gabriel scooped her up and carried her off without another word.

"I—" Sera started, then realized she didn't know what to say. She just felt confused, maybe even a little numb.

"Sera," Kieran said, taking her hand and helping her to her feet. "That's not going to happen. It's okay."

"Prophecies are often figurative, not literal," Kellan said, taking her other hand.

She looked back and forth between them, feeling like a balloon about to burst. She'd only been awake a short time, and already she'd had *too much*. And then there were the two men staring at her with concern, avid heat in their gazes.

"What is this, this connection between us?" she asked, careful to direct the question to both of them.

The twins exchanged a tense look, then shook their heads.

"It's unknowable," Kellan said. "We just have to… sort it out."

Sort it out. An apt choice of words if Sera had ever heard one. There was, it seemed, quite a bit in her life that needed *sorting out*. And if this prophecy was right, she probably didn't have much time to do it.

What the heck had Sera gotten herself into?

CHAPTER 4

"This game is ridiculous," Kellan said with a sigh, jogging and stacking the tiny cards in his hand and placing them face down on the table. He shifted in his seat, trying to keep from rolling his eyes. "Clue? There are many clues, and few answers."

There was a lot Kellan would do in the name of getting to know Sera, but this was a genuine struggle. Losing wasn't something he was good at in the first place, and now he'd lost to both his twin and the girl he fancied. It was... frustrating. Almost as frustrating as sitting across the table from the woman he desired more than anything, playing nice while he and Kieran were both doing their utmost to impress her.

"You're just mad because you haven't won yet," Kieran rejoined. "Sera and I have each won a game apiece, and you're lagging behind."

"You have so many cards," Sera pointed out. "You should have a better chance at this round than either of us."

"He was never much for puzzles, even as a kid," Kieran said with a laugh.

"I can take anything apart and put it back together again. I am fantastic at chess. Poker is almost dangerously easy for me," Kellan said, trying not to get defensive.

Sera reached over and patted his hand.

"It's a game for kids. You're overthinking it," she said, her lush pink lips curving upward in a kind smile. "Just relax and pretend like you're enjoying yourself."

"Did you play this game as a child?" Kieran asked, mercifully drawing the conversation away from Kellan's failure.

"No, definitely not," Sera said, shaking her head. "My parents are very serious people. They're both lawyers and really ambitious and driven. They raised me to be the same. No TV, no pizza parties, no boyfriends. Just studying and school-related activities."

"It sounds like you had quite a boring upbringing," Kellan said, his lips twitching. "Sort of the opposite of Kieran and myself."

"Well," Sera said, laying her cards aside. "I came out of a desperately poor family. My birth parents emigrated to Ireland, and then sort of… lost track of me. Or abandoned me, when I was a baby. Then I was in an orphanage for several years, run by the Catholic Church. My parents went to Cork on vacation one year, and they just happened to ask for directions from a nun at my orphanage. To hear them tell it, I ran out the front door making all kinds of a racket, and ran right into their shins. It took a year, but they brought me home to the States. After all that, maybe a boring childhood was the best thing for me."

"That's quite a story," Kellan said. "I can see why they would want to keep you nice and sheltered. You seem to have turned out all right, after all."

He gave her a wink to let her know he was teasing, and he was rewarded with a blush and a laugh.

"They weren't my jailers or anything," she assured them.

"I ran track, I had friends. Just… studious friends. I wanted to be a doctor from the time I was young, so I just worked toward that single-mindedly."

"How did you end up here, working at Sloane?" Kieran asked.

"Originally I wanted to specialize in pediatrics," she said, tilting her head thoughtfully. "But I had trouble fitting in at human hospitals, all through my residency. So I applied to Kith hospitals all over the country, small and large. Sloane offered me a job doing general medicine, which means I get to do a little of everything. It's challenging and rewarding in equal measure, so I plan to stick around as long as they'll have me."

"It sounds like you've got it all worked out," Kieran replied. "I hate to even ask what your five year plan is, for fear that I'll be vastly outstripped."

"Enough of me answering questions," Sera said, flapping a hand at them. "First, I am going to make a guess at the murderer in the game. Then I want to ask you two questions for a while. Turn the tables."

"Guess away," Kellan said with a sigh.

"Mrs. Plum in the Observatory, with the Rope," she said.

"Damn!" Kieran said, tossing his cards down.

"You didn't even check to see if I was right!" Sera protested.

"I might have taken a peek at the cards earlier," Kieran said with a shrug.

"You… cheater!" she crowed, tossing her cards at him.

"Easy, now. It's all we know," Kieran said with a laugh. "We were raised in the Faerie Court, where it was all lies, intrigue and cutthroat politics. Cheating is how we survived our formative years."

Sera narrowed her eyes, then glanced over at Kellan, as if for affirmation.

"He's right about that bit," Kellan said with a shrug. "The Faerie Court was as brutal as it was wild. We were lucky that the Queen only banished us instead of killing us both."

Kieran snorted.

"Only because she thought you'd come back and be her consort," he said, rolling his eyes.

"Let's talk about something else," Kellan said.

"What? Wait, don't skip over the juicy details!" Sera said, smacking Kellan on the forearm. "You didn't want to be... whatever a consort is in the Faerie realm?"

"Well, for starters, the Queen is our aunt. Also she murdered our entire family, parents and cousins and uncles. And she was quite insane."

"Oh," Sera said, biting her lip. "She... killed your parents?"

"In the bedroom right next to ours," Kieran said, leaning back in his chair and folding his arms. "We were, I think, understandably angry and rebellious as teens."

"And then the Queen kicked you out of the Faerie realm?"

"Yep. Kieran had gotten beaten pretty soundly, so we both landed here in the human realm with nothing but a concussion and the clothes on our backs."

"Where did you go? What did you do?" Sera asked, her eyes wide. The compassion in her made Kellan's heart wrench a little.

"It was centuries ago. We've gone everywhere, tried a little of everything," Kieran said, giving Kellan a look. There were no terrible skeletons in their closets, but the centuries of drinking, gambling, and womanizing weren't really what either twin wanted to tell Sera about. Kellan just arched a brow, knowing his brother would take his expression as one of understanding and agreement.

"So what kind of magic do you guys have? I've never really worked with any Faeries," Sera said.

"Fae," Kellan corrected her. "And we each have different powers. We can use a glamour…"

He summoned a glamour, a bit of magic that transformed his appearance, and made himself look exactly like Mere Marie for just a moment, down to her wild white hair and creamy coffee-colored skin.

"Oh!" Sera squeaked. "That's marvelous."

"We can't hold it for long. We *can* transform into animals, though, and that we can hold almost indefinitely," Kieran added. "Bears, wolves, big cats. Predators, mostly."

"Fascinating," Sera said.

"And then there's the elemental magic," Kellan said. He released the glamour and held his hand out, palm up.

Gentle green wisps of magic blossomed and snaked upward, twisting and climbing like vines until they formed a small green plant. After a moment, a gentle purple bud appeared at the top, then burst into flower before Sera's delighted eyes.

"Here," Kellan said, plucking the bloom from his palm. He leaned over and tucked it behind Sera's ear, and she blushed when his fingers brushed the sensitive skin of her neck.

"Amazing," she breathed.

"My magic is a bit… different," Kieran said, breaking into the moment and earning Kellan's fiercest glare. Kellan could see his twin trying to think of a nice spin to put on his dark powers. Then Kieran grinned, spreading his hands wide, and looked upward.

Snowflakes began to fall, showering them in a gentle layer of soft white powder.

"Holy crap!" Sera said, hand flying to cover her mouth. "That's so cool!"

Kellan rolled his eyes, but Kieran had done his magic masterfully.

"The Light Prince, and the Dark Prince, at your service," he said.

"That's what they called you?" she asked, her brow puckering. She shivered, and Kieran made a gesture that killed the snowfall.

"It is what we are," Kieran said simply, reaching over to brush the snow from her shoulders and hair. "Kellan, warm her up."

Kellan reached out and touched her wrist briefly, sending a burst of warmth through her body. She gave him an appreciative grin.

"Well, this evening has been most illuminating," she said.

Kellan wondered what she meant by that. Was she closer to understanding the Gray brothers, to perhaps choosing which one she wanted more?

Sera yawned and rose from the table.

"Would you two mind packing up the game? I'm a bit tired, and you've given me a lot to think about," she said, stretching.

"Of course," Kellan said. Kieran's expression had gone stormy, but Kellan guessed that his twin was just impatient and hungry, just as Kellan felt.

"Goodnight, then."

Sera headed upstairs to bed, leaving Kellan and Kieran alone.

"The suspense is killing me," Kieran said. "She won't give me the slightest hint as to which of us she is drawn to more strongly. I'm going to go mad with it."

"You and me both," Kellan said as he watched Sera's retreating back.

Sera was a mystery unto herself.

CHAPTER 5

Serafina stood at the stern of the majestic ship the General Goddard, watching the coastline of her native India slowly slip from her view. Behind her, the ship was abustle with the activity of the crew, half a hundred men crawling all over the sails and decks making everything ready for the eight month voyage ahead.

The salty wind whipped her tightly braided hair and tugged at the numerous layers of her clothing. Sera pressed both hands to her stomach, fingers tracing the stiff boning of her corset. She was only just becoming used to the British mode of dress, so different from the comfortable, colorful saris she'd worn her whole life.

She felt cramped and confined in her new garments, but it was for a good cause. She was going to be a British lady, after all, with a fine house in London and all the fripperies that came along with it. A little discomfort could be withstood in order to fit in with her new life.

It was all ahead of her, just as her homeland was behind her.

Sera tilted her head back, inhaling deeply. More than just

the sea air, she could smell the tea and spices that were crammed, cask after cask, into the ship's hold. The aromas of the merchandise that her new husband was taking back to Britain, fulfilling his contracts as a captain in the Honourable East India Company.

"Sera."

She turned to find him standing behind her, looking every bit the title Captain Thomas Foxall in his starched and formal navy uniform. Tall, dark, and handsome, he was everything she'd ever dreamed her future husband could be. That his skin was pale mattered not to her, nor the fact that he insisted that Sera move back to London with him.

She'd go anywhere to be with her beloved Thomas.

"Darling," she said with a smile. She intentionally worked to suppress her accent, copying Thomas's dulcet English tones as best she could.

"Getting better," he said, his eyes sparkling. "You'll be a proper lady by the time we reach the Continent, I should hazard."

"I thought you liked me because I'm a wild heathen," she teased, reaching out to clasp his hand. She wanted to kiss him, but she knew he wouldn't like her to make a scene in front of his men.

Terribly conservative, her Thomas.

"Is all in readiness for when we reach London?" she asked, turning back to watch the dark, shifting water all around the boat.

"My letter announcing our marriage should be arriving within the month," he said with a soft smile, knowing the answer she sought. "I have instructed them to expect a foreigner."

Sera reached up to brush back a lock of dark hair that lay across his forehead, then grinned.

"Perfect."

Thomas opened his mouth to say more, but just then they were interrupted by the cries of a dozen crewmen. Sera couldn't make heads or tails of what they were shouting, but Thomas's whole body went stiff.

"Go belowdecks," he hissed, pulling Sera from the railing and pointing her toward the entrance to the captain's cabin. "Don't leave until I come get you myself."

"What's happening?" Sera cried as he rushed toward the ship's center mast.

She had no need of the answer, because just then a terrific crack rent the air, and the whole ship jolted violently, causing Sera to lose her footing. She grasped the rail with both hands, shaking.

Thomas didn't stop moving, running to the mast and grabbing one of the ship's only floating vests. Even as the thunderous sound of the ship's underbelly cracking and splitting filled the air, he returned to Sera and fitted the vest over her head, cinching it tightly around her.

"If we go down… find a piece of wood that's big enough to support you. I will find you, my love," he told her, his expression serious as the grave.

"Thomas, wait!" she cried as he began to turn away again.

He paused, reaching into his coat, and turned back to her. He grasped her by the waist and kissed her, hard and desperate. When he stepped back once more, Sera felt the cold weight of metal in her hand.

"A pistol?" she asked, confused.

"Do not use it unless no one else is left alive," he told her. "If the ship breaks, I want you to jump and swim as far as you can. Otherwise the ship going down will suck you under. Do you understand?"

Sera could only nod.

Satisfied with that, he whirled and charged toward the ship's bow. Sera tucked the pistol under her floating jacket, then braced herself against the railing again. The great, tall mast that held the ship's sails wavered and tipped away from the rest of the ship, ripping a great crack through the middle of the vessel.

Trembling, Sera knew that she must follow Thomas's instructions, that she must jump and swim as far as she could, even if the ocean's icy black water didn't offer much better chance of survival.

She would not fail him. She would never fail her husband, never.

With shaking hands, Sera pulled herself over the ship's railing and stared down at the inky depths of the water below. She sucked in a deep breath and closed her eyes, sending out the briefest of prayers.

No matter what happens, please let me stay with my Thomas.

Sera braced herself, choked down a sob threatening to wrack her body, and jumped.

Then she was falling, falling, falling....

Sera sucked in a strangled breath, thrashing against her tangled bedsheets. Had she drowned? Had her body broken as she hit the water?

But no, no. She was safe and sound, lying in a warm bed. It took her several long moments to situate herself, but eventually she did. She was staying with the Guardians. She was at the Manor. She was herself, not some sea captain's exotic treasure of a wife.

Flinging the sweat-soaked covers away from her body, she pressed a hand to her pounding heart.

It was just... it had been so *real*. She felt this way sometimes, waking up from dreams about her life in ancient

India, or her life as a sixties housewife in New York. The dreams were always so detailed, so accurate… it was eerie.

But they were just dreams, right? The fact that they reeked of Kith magic, surely that was just a product of her imagination. Wasn't it?

Sinking back against the pillows, Sera closed her eyes and tried to calm her wild heartbeat.

It's nothing, go back to sleep, she chided herself.

Only it didn't feel like nothing…

CHAPTER 6

Kieran had never been so hard up for anything in his long, long life.

Just now, he stared at Sera from the windows of the downstairs lounge as she stood in the backyard chatting with Cassie. Staring her up and down, up and down, admiring every single delicious curve. She wore these amazing jeans that were absolutely *unfair*, and a filmy white shirt that gave just a hint of the dark, lacy lingerie she wore underneath.

"You're drooling," Kellan said, coming up to stand beside him.

"Like you aren't?" Kieran said without taking his eyes from Sera.

She laughed at something Cassie said and tossed her the long, dark chocolate curtain of her hair. She glanced over at Kieran and Kellan, once and then again. Even from this distance, her blush was evident. Kieran could almost smell her arousal every time he was close to her. Goosebumps on her skin, a flush on her cheeks, the way she bit her lip and stared back at him a little too long...

In any other situation, she'd have been in Kieran's bed a week ago, the first night they met.

Instead, he watched from afar, trying to figure out how the hell to fix this situation. As much as he wanted to just sweep Sera off her feet and pleasure her until she lost her breath, there was Kellan to contend with. All week, for every small victory Kieran scored, Kellan was right beside him, neck and neck.

In truth, despite their internal competition, they were also courting Sera, in a way. Trying to learn about her, about her family, her dreams and hopes for the future. About what colors she liked, where she preferred to eat, which Mardi Gras parades she always watched and which she skipped because they were too wild or overcrowded.

The more Kieran found out, the more fascinated he was with her. Aside from being beautiful, aside from being a young doctor, Sera had a lot of interests. She loved children, and volunteered at a childhood vaccination clinic that served the underprivileged community in New Orleans. She liked to walk in City Park on nice days, to feed the fat ducks that floated down the winding little bayous and streams there. She went jogging when we was stressed, or sometimes watched lots and lots of television. *Netflix* and *Gray's Anatomy* were new words in Kieran's vocabulary, thanks to Sera, though he hadn't quite figured either of them out yet.

He and Kellan were going to have to stay on their toes to keep up with quick-thinking Sera and her easy smiles.

In the name of getting to know them both better, Sera had suggested a few activities. Going to the park, checking out the Backstreet Cultural Museum to learn about Mardi Gras Indians, eating out at a wide variety of restaurants. Every step of the way, Kieran and Kellan seemed to be in lockstep, Sera wedged between them.

The night before, they'd strolled through the Gray Market together, each brother showering Sera with little tokens and flowers until she protested the expense of it. Mostly, Kieran intended to introduce Sera around, have her meet some of the people who helped the Guardians in various capacities. She seemed limited in her Kith connections, so of course he wanted to remedy that; he would make her life perfect in every single way, if he could.

The trouble came in introducing her. Everyone they met looked between the three of them, eyes widening a little, and then just rushed through introductions without questioning the situation. Sera had seemed a little embarrassed and disheartened, which frustrated Kieran to no end.

"The trouble is, she's not just pretty," Kellan said absently, cocking his head as he watched her. "The woman is smart, and nice, and funny. Damn her."

Kieran grunted, but he agreed. Serafina Khouri was gorgeous and charming on a number of levels, and keeping himself in check around her was proving exceptionally difficult. Not punching Kellan's teeth in was also a constant struggle, especially when he found his brother staring at Sera with a downright explicit expression on his face.

"It's funny, you know. All our lives, we've only had each other. And now... we're each standing in the way of the other's happiness. If you didn't exist, or I didn't exist... Happy mateship, burgeoning family. None of the lies or melodrama from our life at the Summer Court. It would be..." he paused, searching for the right word.

"Idyllic," Kellan finished for him.

Kieran arched a brow.

"I loathe you when you finish my sentences," he informed his brother.

Kellan gave an amused snort, but just turned to stare at Sera again.

"Something has to break," Kellan said after a minute. "I can't stand this anymore. And Sera seems frozen, terrified. She might be attracted to us both, but she can never get close enough to love one of us like this."

"Love," Kieran repeated absently. "There's the crux, I suppose."

"Every time one of us snarls or snaps at the other, she fades a little more, I think."

"And your solution is… what?" Kieran challenged.

"A truce. Let her choose one of us based on our true selves, not because one of us bullies the other more effectively."

Kieran frowned, thinking. He could follow his brother's thinking, but he had to wonder. When it came down to their true selves, how different were they really? Two halves of a whole, and they'd known it from their first breath. If they could barely differentiate themselves, how could they expect Sera to make that kind of choice?

Still, a truce would be the best thing for Sera. A little charm and fun to balance out the tension of the last week… yeah, letting off a little steam was probably just the ticket.

"Shake on it?" he said, thrusting a hand out.

Kellan shook it, a glimmer of amusement in his green eyes. Neither of them gave in to the temptation to grip the other's hand until it hurt, and Kieran was proud of them both for a brief moment.

"How about we go get a drink at Cure?" he suggested.

"You read my mind," Kellan said. "She'll like it."

Kieran nodded, wondering at the slow shift in his twin and in himself. *She'll like it* had never been a reason either of them did anything, ever. He blew out a breath.

"You go tell her, huh?" he offered.

Kellan didn't hesitate, just flashed Kieran a smirk and headed toward Sera.

If nothing else, this evening would certainly prove interesting. Could Kieran and Kellan keep their rivalry and jealousy at bay for even a single night?

Call it an experiment.

CHAPTER 7

"Do me a favor?" Kieran asked Sera, leaning in close to keep his words private.

The bar they'd chosen was a hip Uptown place, all dark walls, gleaming bottles and posh young customers. It was booming tonight. When Sera mentioned wanting to find a place to sit, the brothers had been forced to intimidate a whole flock of twenty-something guys in button-ups to get this tiny corner booth. She'd gotten her wish, and now she was pressed tightly between Kieran and Kellan as she sipped her elegant-looking champagne cocktail.

"What's that?" Sera said, her ruby-tinged lips curling up into a smile.

"Only ever wear that dress," he suggested, reaching down to tug the thigh-length hem. The white silk cocktail dress set off her skin and revealed her fantastic legs and cleavage to full advantage. "Or... well, wearing nothing at all would also be acceptable."

He winked at her, and had to smother a laugh. He could almost hear Kellan's eye roll. Kellan had done well enough tonight, engaging Sera about books and classic films. Kieran flirted with her, and talked to her about bands they both liked.

Then there were the cocktails... with each drink, the lines between Kieran and Kellan and even Sera seemed to blur a little more. It felt... relaxing? Satisfying? Whatever it was, Kieran wasn't about to interrupt with questions.

As the night grew later and the champagne and whiskey flowed, the bar's lights seemed to dim more and more until their booth began to feel more than cozy. Private, almost. Kieran could see Kellan's hand resting on Sera's knee, just as Kieran had thrown his arm over her shoulder. Intimate, daring.

Sera was explaining a situation she had to deal with at work, a coworker who blatantly sexually harassed her and then didn't take her rejection very well.

"He's just... it's like he's brainwashed all the nurses, just because he's good looking," Sera said, downing the last drops in her champagne flute and grimacing. "It's so frustrating. Sorry to complain about my job, but it's driving me nuts."

"Do you want us to kill him?" Kieran asked, only half joking.

Sera sputtered and blotted at her lips with a napkin, eyes widening.

"I don't think that will be necessary," she said, but his comment did the trick.

"It made you smile though, thinking of his death," Kieran pointed out with no little humor.

"I was laughing at your offer, not his death!" Sera protested. "That's awful."

She pulled a face, as if she wasn't entirely certain of her words. Kieran and Kellan both laughed and Kieran signaled the waitress for another round as they all sank back in the booth with a collective sigh.

"Can I ask you both a question?" Sera asked, nibbling her lower lip.

"Of course," Kellan replied. Kieran merely crossed his arms and waited.

"Why aren't either of you mated?" she asked, looking between them.

They both stumbled for a moment over that one, grins faltering.

"It's complicated," Kellan said. "With the fated mates stuff. Plus we both travel so much, it's not like either of us was seeking…"

He trailed off, perhaps realizing that his statement wasn't going anywhere particularly lighthearted.

"So you believe in the fated mates thing, then," Sera said, bobbing her head thoughtfully. "What about you, Kieran?"

Kieran sucked in a breath and let it out slowly, formulating his response.

"I do as well. Rather, I believe in it fully now that I've met you. Before, I more used it as a reason not to get close to women," he admitted with a shrug. "A lot of unmated Kith are notoriously promiscuous… Using the excuse of some unknown future mate is a good way to justify that."

Sera arched a brow.

"How honest of you," she said, her tone easy. None of the sarcasm or judgment he would have expected with a less mature woman. Sera, despite her youth, lacked the entitlement and harshness Kieran had encountered with some of her peers. It was even more impressive considering that she had to be ambitious and driven to get her M.D., yet she'd lost none of her compassion or kindness.

Kieran couldn't help himself as Sera gazed up at him, that sweetness shining in her eyes. He leaned down and brushed his lips against hers, ever so gently. Her soft intake of breath said she was surprised, and when he brushed his thumb against her wrist he could feel her heartbeat thrumming like a rabbit's.

Color rose in her cheeks and she pulled back, glancing at Kellan. For a moment, Kieran's heart squeezed painfully when he saw the raw want in her eyes, the hunger and desire for his twin.

Then Sera spoke, and rocked his entire world.

"What if... what if I want both of you?" she asked, her voice so quiet that Kieran almost lost it in the pounding beat of the music. She ducked her head a little, as if ashamed of her own appetite.

Kellan glanced up at Kieran for the barest moment, a look full of a hundred tiny thoughts. Kieran only nodded, knowing what Kellan was thinking.

Sera wouldn't be the first woman they'd shared in this way, at the same time...

Kieran pulled Sera onto his lap even as Kellan surged forward, kissing her deeply, digging his fingers into her hair. Sera went rigid against Kieran for the briefest second, then surrendered with a moan. Kieran pulled her hair back and teased her earlobe with his lips, chuckling when one of her hands clutched at his knee, nails digging into his skin through his jeans.

Yes, sweet little Sera was already quite perfect. Like she was made for this, made for both of them.

If only that were possible...

A knot of tension tightened in Kieran's chest, but he forced the sensation away. He was touching Sera, tasting the salty-sweet skin of her neck as he kissed and nipped at her, drawing soft sighs from her lips. Her delectable ass pressed into his lap, teasing his already-hard cock. His hand wandered up to cup her full breast through her shirt and bra, all worries forgotten.

When his clever fingers found her nipple, giving it a soft

pinch, Sera broke the kiss with Kellan and threw her head back with a soft cry. Kieran glanced at Kellan, arching a brow. His twin took over fondling her breasts, kissing the top of both creamy mounds where they spilled over the tight neckline of her dress.

As Kellan took her lips again in a fierce kiss, Kieran adjusted the tablecloth to make sure she was completely hidden from the view of any onlookers and then began to edge the hem of her dress up, up, up her bare thighs. She tensed a little when he slid his fingers down the inside of her thigh, seeking, pushing aside the silky front of her panties. He brushed her slit with two fingertips, finding and circling her clit, and she gave a shaky moan.

"Think what we would do to you if we were in the privacy of the bedroom," Kieran whispered in her ear. She shivered against him, her hands coming up to dig into the fine silvering hair at the nape of Kellan's neck. "You're so hot, so sensitive. What would you feel if I used my lips here?"

He gave her clit a soft pinch and she trembled, arching against Kieran to thrust her breasts harder against Kellan's hands, rocking her hips softly against Kieran's hand. All her inhibitions abandoned; she was wild and wanting. Her excitement made Kieran burn, he knew she ached just as he did now.

"Would you like it if one of us was inside you while the other sucks on your nipples? What if one of us takes you here," he said, sliding his fingers lower to tease her slick entrance, "and the other takes your mouth? Would you like that, sweet Sera? I think you would."

The second his fingertips found her clit again Sera exploded, her whole body shaking. Kellan swallowed her cries and kissed her desperately. Kieran massaged her thighs for a moment before he righted her garments. Sera broke from her kiss with Kellan, turning and kissing Kieran. Their tongues met, giving Kieran a quick glimpse of her sweet taste as Kellan ran his hands up and down her arms, soothing and comforting, letting her know she was well cared-for.

She pulled back and leaned against them both, brushing her tousled hair away from her face.

"Is this what it would be like? All three of us, like this?" she asked, still a little breathless.

"What do you mean, darling?" Kellan asked, dropping a kiss on her head.

"If we are meant to be mates, all three of us. Would it be like this?"

Kieran's heart locked up, his muscles froze. His gaze snapped to Kellan's, and he knew his twin was thinking the same thing.

All three of us? Share her, forever?

And then: *fuck, no.*

"No," Kellan told her, his voice deceptively soft. Kieran could nearly feel his brother's anger radiating outward, but Sera's eyes drifted closed for a moment, and she seemed none the wiser. "You'll have to choose, Sera."

Her eyes opened as suddenly as the slamming of a door.

"What if I don't want to?" she asked, her brow creasing.

Kellan's expression turned murderous. He picked up the glass tumbler with the remnants of his whisky and shot it back, slamming the glass on the table when finished.

"We all want things we can't have, darling," Kellan said. Rising and pulling out his wallet, he tossed a handful of cash on the table. A ridiculous gesture, since Kieran had a tab open at the bar. "I have to go patrol. I'll see you back at the Manor."

Kellan leaned down and pressed his lips to Sera's briefly, his gaze connecting with Kieran's. He was *furious*. A heartbeat later he was gone, vanished into the night.

"I don't understand," Sera said, her voice plaintive.

Kieran did. All too well, but he had no pretty words to give her.

"Let's go home," he suggested, taking her hand. After all, what else was there to say? When it came down to it, facts were facts.

Sera would have to choose.

CHAPTER 8

Sera sat in an overstuffed chair in what Kieran and Kellan insisted on calling her bedroom, knees tucked up to her chin as she stared out the big bay window. The afternoon sun slanted in, warming her skin, but she longed to be outside. Her mind and body were both restless, and she knew just where to lay the blame.

Kieran and Kellan had swooped in and fawned over her for a week straight, giving her insane amounts of attention, like she was the single most important person in the whole universe. Then there was last night…

Her cheeks burned just thinking about it. Right there in the bar, though she didn't think anyone saw… The way they'd both touched her, teased her, tasted her… Goosebumps broke out on her skin just thinking about what Kieran and Kellan had made her feel, made her do…

And then Kellan threw down the gauntlet, telling her to choose. Between two men who charmed and delighted her, who made her heart beat fast, who set her on fire?

Huffing a sigh, she got up and started pulling on her running gear. After a week at the Manor, the sumptuous but impersonal guest bedroom had grown overwhelming. She'd finally made the twins take her to her apartment in MidCity to retrieve some of her more important possessions, like running shoes and extra lab coats for work.

Hell or high water, Sera was going back to work in a couple of days. She was dying of boredom lying around the Manor like a spoiled Victorian lady. Plus, it was a waste of good doctor skills for her to be cooped up here all day! In addition to returning to work, she'd flat-out told Kellan that she was going to start running again, for her mental health more than anything.

Stuck here between the two men, Sera couldn't *think*.

Sufficiently dressed, Sera tucked a few bucks in the waistband of her shorts, put in her earbuds, and headed downstairs. She spent a couple minutes stretching in the front yard, then left the Manor's boundaries at an easy lope. When she passed through the outer barrier of the wards, she felt them slither over her skin and tug at her, as if unwilling to release her.

Creepy.

She shook it off and headed toward the Marigny, thinking to head into the lower part of the French Quarter and people watch as she went. Maybe stop for a special treat, since she'd been stuck indoors all week?

Her thoughts followed her, refusing to be outrun, nipping at her heels with every step.

Choose. Choose. Choose.

What if I don't want to choose?! she growled at the persistent voice in the back of her head. *What if, one time in my life, I just want it all, without sacrificing anything?*

She slowed to a walk near Cafe du Monde, entering the line for a small cafe au lait and a beignet. As she sipped her coffee and nibbled at the powered doughnut, she sat on a concrete ledge to watch people walk by. Every color, race, creed, size, style, and age walked right by on their way to various places in the French Quarter.

She was so absorbed in her doughnut that it took her a minute to feel the gaze on her back. When she turned a little to her left, she found a wizened-looking older gentleman sitting only a few feet away, staring at her. Magic poured from his aura, conflicting with his unassuming looks, but he merely smiled at her and kept staring.

"Um, hello," she said, wiping at the powdered sugar on her lips.

"It's been a lifetime since I've seen one of your kind," was his odd response. "Never thought to see one again, either. Thought y'all were extinct, if you don't mind me saying."

"I'm sorry?" Sera asked. For a horrifying moment, she thought maybe he was talking about her Middle Eastern looks.

"A phoenix, dear. You're the first I've seen since the rise of Christianity." His lips curved into a happy smile.

"I— what?" Sera was beyond confused.

"I thought you'd look different," he said, his tone perfectly conversational. "The other one, he was a big warrior. I saw him burn, even. It was magnificent!"

"I think you have me confused," Sera said, standing up and brushing herself off. "Have a nice day, okay?"

"Be careful, little bird. You don't believe me, but there are dark creatures who will recognize you. They will see what I see, and they will want to use you. Powerful, you phoenixes."

"Sir—"

"You ever have one of those... what do they call it... deja vu moments?" he asked, tilting his head as he examined her. "But more. You live another life, another century, another everything?"

Sera's mouth opened to say *no*, then closed.

"Maybe," she managed.

"That's because of what you are, little bird. You burn and rise, and burn again. And now… well, I should think you're a little long in the tooth for a phoenix. Any day now, my dear. Gather ye rosebuds while ye may," he said, waving a hand.

"Well… thanks?" she said with a strangled laugh.

"Anytime," he said with a conspiratorial wink. Then he turned his face up, as if scenting the wind. "You ought to get moving, little bird. Someone's coming, someone looking for you."

"Have a nice day," Sera said, already moving.

His words chilled her to the bone. As interesting as the idea of her lineage was, his warnings had put her on edge. Every inch of her skin tingled with some kind of premonition as she broke into a jog, turning around and heading through the French Market. Just as she picked up her pace, she passed a strange man in a dark trench coat. He made direct and blatant eye contact with Sera for a second. Out of the corner of her eye, she saw him follow when she started moving faster.

"Shit."

Sera broke into a flat run, raising her hand to flag down a taxi that was moving in the same direction. Typical New Orleans taxi driver, he screeched to a halt and let Sera climb in without question. Sera struggled to catch her breath all the way back to the Manor, shoving a handful of bills at the driver as she raced into the now-welcoming wards that protected the house.

She didn't stop running until she was all the way up the stairs. She burst into her bedroom, heart pounding, and came to a grinding halt.

Kieran and Kellan stood right there, arms crossed… and they looked *pissed*.

"Uh… hey," she said, leaning down, trying to catch her breath. "Went for… a run…"

"Duverjay saw you get out of a cab," Kellan said, his words accusatory.

Sera's gaze narrowed. Just because they had this thing between them didn't mean he could just go around making decisions for her, accusing her of things. Making ultimatums, especially. Sera was her own woman.

"I got a cramp," she lied, glad she was already flushed from her run. She was a terrible liar, but her breathlessness covered it up this time.

"Are you okay?" Kieran asked, moving to her side. As if he was going to… what, sweep her up and carry her to bed? Over a cramp? Kira had been right about the Guardians, they were overbearing alpha males.

"I'm fine," she said, dropping onto the chair beside her bed. "I just needed a little exercise, needed to clear my head. It helped."

"Helped?" Kellan still watched her like a hawk. A skeptical hawk, that was.

"Decide," she said, giving them both a placid look. "You told me to decide, remember?"

The way they glanced at each other, throats working nervously, made her wish she hadn't taken such a rude tone with them. She softened her tone for the next part, the part where she would give them both what they wanted… sort of.

"I don't want to choose between you. I want you both. I think that's what is supposed to happen, otherwise we wouldn't feel this way." She paused and let that sink in for a moment before continuing, "Both, or neither. No more fighting, no more competition. You didn't think I missed that, did you?"

The incredulous look that passed between them made her want to laugh, but she held it in. This was a serious moment.

"I feel the same draw for both of you. Maybe it's not what I always pictured, having two men in my life. But more than anything, I always wanted a big family, lots of faces around the dinner table or fireplace or what have you. Maybe this is just… part of what I need. And since we're fated, maybe it's what you both need, too."

"Sera—" Kieran started. One glance at the hard lines of his facial expression, and Sera stopped him.

"Nope," she said, standing and shooing them toward the door. "Both of you out, please. Take some time to think about what I said. I need a nice long shower."

The second they were in the hallway, she gently closed the door to their surprised faces.

Yep, I just did that.

All Sera could do now was hope that they'd do the right thing, for all their sakes.

CHAPTER 9

Kellan sat at the far end of The John, his favorite utterly shitty dive bar, knocking back shots of tequila. The fact that he was drinking tequila was a bad, bad sign. Kellan plus tequila never went well, without exception. It was the gateway to his angry, lonely place, the place he went when life was just pissing in his eye.

And the hangover from the tequila? Salt in the wound. Still he drank and brooded, even smoking half a cigar before growing disgusted with it and stubbing it out on the ground. The John was all cement floors and metal chairs, the kind of scuzzy place that they likely cleaned with a firehose at the end of the night. It had a certain atmosphere, which suited Kellan's mood.

I'm not going to choose, she'd said.

Fuuuuuuck. Her words had completely floored him. Worse, he understood her side of things even as jealousy raged within his chest, ripping and tearing at his ego and his heart. So he drank and moped, needing some time away from Sera and Kieran. He especially didn't need Sera to see this side of him, this childish competitiveness and selfishness that he couldn't seem to ever get over.

He knew better, damn it. He knew what he needed to do, the words he needed to say. But he kept imagining the grin that Kieran would give him, the same one Kieran had every single time he stole one of Kellan's bed partners or somehow got one over on him. That cocky, shit-eating, unrepentant grin that made Kellan see fucking red. Every. Single. Time.

Since their childhood, the twins had been pitted against each other. Once their individual brands of magic had been discovered, Kieran had been the instant black sheep, the Dark Prince. It was unfair, and Kellan had been the first to stick up for him, but then Kieran did what he did best: he turned it to a kind of advantage.

He'd taunted Kellan, saying that the Dark Prince was much stronger than the Light, that Kellan was a coddled little baby, all the stuff that would give a young boy a stiff upper lip. Then they fought, beating the crap out of each other, and eventually the whole argument was forgotten.

Until the next time someone brought up the Light and the Dark. Always, Kieran internalized the whole thing. Always, he turned it into a fight between the brothers, rather than a hurtful comment from an outsider. It should have been the two Princes against the world, the Gray brothers versus everyone else.

Instead, Kieran chose to fight Kellan. Using his reputation as the faster, looser, and more dangerous brother, Kieran plucked women, cars, and jobs out of Kellan's hands. Anything Kellan was given, anything he worked for... it didn't matter. Kieran wanted it, and he took it.

Worse, women often wanted to leave Kellan for Kieran. Kellan was safe, boring, emotional, messy... Kieran was exciting, dashing, heart-stopping. It drove Kellan mad. It also drove the brothers apart again and again, fighting and separating before eventually drifting back together.

Kellan turned the past over and over in his mind, trying to grasp the slippery part... did the past actually matter? Were they doomed to repeat it, or could they break the cycle? Would Sera be the thing that changed them, saved them, or would she be just another tragedy that left Kellan raw inside?

At that, Kellan paused and eyed the bottle of tequila before him. That last bit sounded more like the booze talking than him, and the half-empty bottle backed up his theory. Tequila gave him melodramatic tendencies.

"You seem like a man with a lot of troubles."

Kellan turned to find a thin, balding man sitting two stools down the bar, sipping a can of cheap beer. The guy was Kith, but not very powerful. Maybe some low-level mage or something.

"You seem like a stranger with a lot of opinions," Kellan told him, expecting his harsh words to shut down the conversation before it could really start. But no, the guy was a chatty drunk.

"No offense, no offense," he said, staring straight ahead instead of looking at Kellan. "Just, you know, we all have problems. There are always more solutions than we know, you know?"

Kellan merely grunted, finishing the last of the shot he'd poured and then pushing the shot glass away. He pulled out his wallet, ready to pay and leave.

"Listen," the stranger started up again. "I think I can help you, friend."

Kellan paused, a wad of cash in his hand, and turned the full force of his glare on the guy. The other guy cringed before Kellan even spoke.

"We are *not* friends," Kellan spat. "And I am not someone you want to fuck with, I assure you."

"I can solve your problem, though," the guy insisted, though he grew paler with each word. "The problem with your, uh, mate. I can clear the path for you to have her, *alone*."

A fission of red sizzled through Kellan's veins.

"Are you threatening my brother?" he asked, keeping his tone calm. "Are you with Papa Aguiel?"

"No no," the guy said, raising his hands and turning to Kellan at last. "Call me a… concerned third party. Or my boss is, anyway. My boss recruits big guys like you, mercenary style. Rewards his soldiers beyond their wildest dreams."

"And what the fuck does this have to do with me?" Kellan asked, letting his teeth show on the last. "Quickly, you are starting to annoy me."

He raised a hand, powering a spell. White mist began to seep into the darkened bar, creeping across the floor and climbing up itself like ivy to create a little cage around the stranger. The guy broke into a sweat, but to his credit he kept going. It made Kellan very curious about who this guy's boss might be.

"Look, we just got a tip that the Light and Dark Princes were here, and that they were in such a circumstance that one of them might be looking for a way out. We pay well, the work's hard and fun, and the members are tight as brothers. It's just an offer. Voluntary, 100%. But if you were to whisper it in your brother's ear, say…"

"Don't approach me again. And if you come anywhere near me or my family, it'll be the last thing you ever do." Kellan stood and tossed his money on the bar.

"If you change your mind," the guy said, thrusting a business card at Kellan. "Get tired of sharing… we have big plans, and your brother would fit in well with our organization. Hell, so would you, for that matter. One of you bows out, the other gets the pretty doctor all to himself…"

Kellan snarled and bucked at the guy, who turned tail and

fled without another word, beer can abandoned on the bar. Kellan looked down at the card in his hand.

les mercenaires
t. 504.000.0000

"The Mercenaries," he read, then grunted. The phone number didn't even look real. And why the hell was it in French, anyway?

For half a moment, he let himself imagine what would happen if Kieran *bowed out*, as the guy had suggested. Kellan and Sera, walking hand in hand. A marriage ceremony, like some humans liked to have. Sera holding a child, *their* child, and gazing up at Kellan lovingly…

Kellan forced the fantasy away, guilt flooding him instantly. There had to be some solution, like the stranger had said, but this wasn't it.

What else was left, though?

Kellan sat up in his bed, a chill crawling down his spine.

Wrong. It couldn't be…

He'd gone to bed drunk, embarrassingly so. Then he'd dreamt. Of Sera, of kissing and touching her. Of her waving goodbye to him as she walked away, hand in hand with Kieran. And then he dreamt of his brother, alone.

In the last bit of his dream, Kellan had waded through an icy lake, the water up to his waist. Kieran was in his arms, as cold and placid as the lake water. On and on Kellan went, looking for help, for somewhere to lay down his burden. Kieran grew heavier by the moment, the water colder, threatening to freeze Kellan's heart.

Still on and on he went, no light, no dark, just... endlessness. Numbness.

Finally he saw a dark figure, standing on the shore of the lake. Waiting. Kellan stopped and squinted, trying to make out the figure's face. Though he didn't know Papa Aguiel on sight, for some reason Kellan *knew* that this figure was his enemy. In that way of dreams, knowing without knowing. Time without comprehension. Fear without stimulus.

Kellan knew he could not take Kieran ashore, because Papa Aguiel wanted him to do just that. But then, as he watched, too afraid to move, he saw Sera. She stood, expression blank, looking out at Kellan without recognition. As if he meant nothing, as if they'd never met.

Papa Aguiel tossed back his head and laughed, his teeth flashing white in the blurry darkness of his shape. He held out his hand to Sera without speaking. She took it, docile, and let Papa Aguiel lead her away from the lake.

"Sera!"

Her name was on his lips as he woke. The chill of the dream, of Kieran's cold and lifeless skin against his own, clung to him even after he pulled the covers up over his body.

It had been surreal, nothing like life.

And yet... too real. The feeling of it, of losing his twin, of losing his mate...

That had been unimaginable, though brief.

It could not happen.

Kellan wouldn't let it.

CHAPTER 10

"This is chaos," Kieran said. He braced as Gabriel took the SUV around a tight turn at top speed, turning around in the passenger seat to see what was happening behind him in the back seat. Sera was on one side, Kellan on the other, and Cassie was in the middle looking white as a sheet.

"Shut the fuck up," Gabriel snarled as he rocketed the car toward the entrance to Sloane General. "When it's your baby, we can have this conversation again."

Kieran shut his mouth, glancing back again. Sera held one of Cassie's hands, Kellan the other as the SUV squealed to a stop near the ER's entrance. The second the car was no longer in motion, Kieran and Gabriel opened the back doors, Gabriel shouldering Kellan out of the way in order to scoop his mate up and carry her through the bolt-hole portal himself.

"She's so nervous," Sera said as Kieran ushered her through into the cool white hallway of the Kith hospital. "First babies are always scary."

That was the last exchange he had with Sera for a good

long while. From then forward, she was in full doctor mode, bustling around and getting Cassie set up in a delivery room. While Gabriel was allowed to stay with Cassie, the other Guardians and their mates were relegated to a nearby waiting room. After that, Kieran only got glances of Sera from time to time. Once, she popped her head in just to update everyone.

"Everything's going swimmingly!" she said brightly. "No baby yet, but soon."

And then she was gone. Her demeanor was cheerful but professional, calm but enthusiastic. She was in her element, that much was utterly certain. Sera was meant to be a doctor, it was plain as day. Mostly it was a lot of hurry up and wait, it seemed.

After the rush to get to the hospital, the baby took its sweet time entering the world. Everyone sipped crappy hospital coffee and watched late night TV, and waited. Kieran kept catching Echo giving Rhys weird, excited smiles. Something was happening there, he was pretty sure of it.

Was Echo anticipating that she and Rhys would be in that very delivery room in the not-so-distant future? The furtive glances and happy blushing said *maybe*.

"We've got a baby!" Gabriel bellowed, rushing into the room.

Everyone jumped to their feet and cheered. There was a lot of hugging, even Kieran and Kellan. The mood was contagious, irresistible. Gabriel announced that it was a girl and then disappeared again, and everyone milled around excitedly.

Soon enough, Sera reappeared, beaming from ear to ear.

"You guys want to come meet the new addition?" she asked, radiating happiness.

She led everyone into the delivery room. Cassie was propped up in the bed, looking exhausted but cheerful.

Gabriel hovered over her, looking so proud he might burst. And in Cassie's arms was the tiniest, reddest baby Kieran had ever seen.

"This is Marie," Cassie said shyly, pulling back a bit of the blanket to show the baby off.

Echo and Alice were outright crying, Kira clung to Asher like an anchor, and all the Guardians were clapping each other on the back like they'd done something wonderful. It was ridiculous, but little Marie was indeed miraculous.

"Where's her namesake?" Asher asked.

"Mere Marie is holding down the fort at the Manor. She'll come visit the baby once some of us are there to take her place," Rhys informed him.

Sera went over and cooed over the baby, which made something in Kieran's heart wrench. He snagged Kellan's arm and towed his twin over to the corner for a conference.

"This could be our life," Kieran said.

Kellan arched a questioning brow.

"Our, like all three of us," Kieran clarified. "If we'd just shake hands and stop trying to piss circles around Sera."

Kellan was silent for a beat, then he nodded.

"Agreed."

"It won't be easy, but it's what Sera deserves. Maybe fate knows what she's doing."

"I was thinking along the same lines, actually," Kellan admitted.

"We'll mark her together?" Kieran asked.

"Tonight," Kellan said, looking grave. "Shake on it?"

They clasped hands, then embraced. When they broke apart, Sera watched them with a great deal of interest.

"We should let Cass here get some rest," Sera announced a few minutes later. "Dr. Bristol is taking really good care of her, and Gabriel will be here too. The rest of us should clear out."

"I could use a nap," Cassie said, and everyone chuckled.

A line formed to congratulate the happy couple one more time, and then everyone filed out. All the couples broke up instinctually, leaving Kieran, Kellan, and Sera standing in the waiting room.

"Well?" she asked, her voice turning teasing. "Who's going to give me a ride home? Or are we just going to stand here?"

"We both are," Kellan said, holding out a hand to her.

She hesitated.

"It's time to go home," Kieran said when she glanced at him. He reached out and took her hand, Kellan taking the other.

Sera bit her lip, looking back and forth between them, a question written in her big brown eyes.

Kieran and Kellan nodded as one, and both chuckled when Sera's knees gave out.

"You've got to stop fainting around us," Kellan teased.

"Let's get you out of here," Kieran said.

Hand in hand with Sera, he led their triad out of the hospital and toward the biggest decision of their lives.

CHAPTER 11

Sera couldn't help but feel a little nervous on the way home. Kellan and Kieran were silent the whole ride home. Kieran drove and Kellan gave Sera the passenger seat. They didn't even look at each other, and the tension in the car bloomed until Sera couldn't take it anymore.

She reached out and flipped on the radio, blinking in surprise when rap blared out of the car's speakers. It made her wonder which of the Guardians was partial to rap, since one of them must have selected the station. They were all so rigid and controlled, she couldn't imagine most of them choosing that type of music.

Asher, maybe? Since Asher was only something like mid-thirties and had lived a human lifespan so far, maybe he was young enough to appreciate it, unlike the rest of the Guardians.

Before Sera knew it, they were back at the Manor. She started to open her door and get out of the car, only to find Kellan opening the door for her. He grabbed her by the waist and laid her over his shoulder, ignoring her protests.

"Guys! Guys, I can walk!" she said.

She appreciated their commitment to getting her into bed, really she did, but there was no need for them to both jog up the stairs with her in tow, was there? That said, she did get a glorious view of Kieran's perfectly shaped ass all the way up the stairs, so...

She'd call it a draw.

When Kellan set her down on the bed, she looked between them and licked her lips, her mouth suddenly quite dry. Both of them stood before her, tall and broad and ruggedly-shaped, expressions more intense than she'd seen before.

Sera bit her lip, summoning all her courage to say what was in her heart.

"There's something we need to talk about before we get any closer to... all this," she said, gesturing toward the bed.

Kieran and Kellan's twin expressions of confusion were almost laughable, if the moment weren't quite so serious.

"You can tell us anything," Kellan said, reaching out and snagging her hand.

"This is less to do with me, and more to do with you two. I told you I wanted you both, and I meant it. And I understand if you two need boundaries, if you don't want to share every moment with me for the rest of your lives. But if you two tell me you're willing to share our lives, to be a family..." Sera hesitated, rubbing the back of her neck. "I need to know that you two are serious, that you want to be part of this as much as I do. Together."

"Of course we do," Kieran said, but the glance he gave Kellan made Sera's stomach do an odd flip.

"Don't rush into this, guys," Sera insisted. "You have to want this, really want all three of us to be together. What if we do start a family? We might not know... whose child is whose, specifically. You know? Can you guys handle that? Or will you both compete for the rest of our lives? I can't watch you fight over every little thing for decades to come. I won't."

"Sera, that isn't an issue," Kieran said, his tone sharper than Sera liked. She arched her brows and crossed her arms, eyeing them both.

Kellan turned from Sera to Kieran, a softly bitter twist to his lips.

"Don't make this about the past," Kellan said.

"I'm not. It's not," Kieran said, sounding defensive. He glanced at Sera, as if worried that she was going to see something she shouldn't, more than he wanted to let her see.

"This is what I'm talking about," Sera said. "The two of you have been two halves of a whole for so long, you can't let me in. We have to become three pieces of the same puzzle if this is ever going to work."

Kieran's whole body was tense, his fists clenched, his jaw rigid.

"You don't understand," he said.

"No? So tell me," Sera said.

Kieran looked at Kellan, who was nearly as tightly wound as his twin.

"Tell her," Kellan said, shaking his head. "If this is what's holding us back, she deserves to know."

Kieran just stared at Kellan with a stony expression.

"Fine. I'll tell her, then." Kellan sighed and turned to Sera. "When we were young, we were pitted against each other. The Faerie Court is a dangerous place, and everything is ruled by politics. Kieran and I were victims of that system, from birth."

"But why? What do children care about politics?" Sera asked.

"Our grandparents were the Queen Regent and the Prince Consort for aeons, and then they passed away suddenly. Their death was suspicious, but the Court was too wound up about choosing a successor to care. Our mother was second in line to the throne, and our Aunt Maeve third."

"So when you said your parents were killed…" Sera asked.

"By our own family, no less," Kieran said, finally adding his bit. "After they died, we learned not to trust anyone except for each other."

"The important thing to understand about our upbringing is that the tragedy was inevitable, in a way. Two strong Fae Princes, each with a unique set of powers. Life and death, a perfect balance. Together, we can do nearly anything."

"And people were threatened by that, I'm guessing?" Sera asked.

"Damn right," Kieran said, looking grim. "The only way to keep us from dominating the entire Faerie Court was to drive a wedge between us. From the time I understood words, I knew that I was the Dark Prince, and Kellan the Light. He was good, I was bad."

"They told me I was weak, that Kieran would always be strong, always control me," Kellan said.

Kieran gave Kellan a surprised look.

"They said that to you?" he asked.

"Even Father, yes. Mother was the only one who ever told me we were equal," Kellan said, an old anger simmering in his gaze.

Kieran snorted, shaking his head.

"They told me that I was weaker, because I couldn't create life. I could only take it, taint it." His amusement was black as night. "The bastards. Playing with kids like that. It was cruel."

"But you brought it into the human realm with you," Sera reminded him gently.

"We never meant to," Kellan said earnestly. "It's just… our whole young lives, we were raised to compare ourselves, to compete. Being identical twins only made it worse, since success or rejection couldn't be based on something as shallow as our looks, or something like a natural ability."

"Yeah. If one of us wins over the other, it's genuinely because one of us isn't good enough. One is better than the other," Kieran said, looking at his brother.

"Eventually we began a very long, very quiet war. We both fought to be the favored brother, in any and every scenario."

There was a long moment of silence.

"I imagine that the small grievances and hurts start to pile up over time. Especially when you've been together for almost a thousand years," Sera surmised.

Both brothers dipped their heads, and she could sense their hurt and shame. Sera reached out and took both their hands, squeezing them tightly.

"You two are wonderful, each on your own merits. I care for you equally, and neither of you will ever mean more to me than the other. Perhaps I should say, I promise that you will both be my favorite mate," Sera said, trying to bring some humor into the situation. "If you two honestly want this, the way that I want this, you will have to decide that for yourselves. Can you live knowing that you will share not only a mate, but a family and a future together?"

The twins were silent, staring at each other intently.

"More importantly," Sera said, "Can you forgive each other? Here and now, start over. Leave the past behind and start a new path, hand in hand with me."

She started to pull her hands from theirs, thinking to give them a few moments of privacy to talk. To her surprise, neither man would release her from their grip.

"No," Kieran said to Sera, without looking away from Kellan. "You're our mate. You need to be here."

Sera stilled, waiting. Seconds ticked by, then a full minute. Finally, Kieran spoke again.

"I forgive you. I absolve you, Kellan."

His words rang through Sera's head and heart, filling her with joy.

"And I you, Kieran. Of everything, for everything. We start anew, right now."

Sera's eyes filled with tears as she stared up at them.

"Thank you," she whispered. "Thank you both. I am the luckiest woman in the world."

"We would do anything for you," Kellan said. "We want to complete the bond with you more than either of us has ever wanted anything, I think."

Both brothers turned their gazes on her at the same time, and Sera's whole body began to heat with slow, simmering anticipation.

"I don't really…" she said, then hesitated. "I don't know how to start."

"Sera," Kieran grated, reaching down and taking her hand. He turned her palm face up and placed a searing kiss against her inner wrist. "What do you want? You want to touch me? Touch me, then."

He brought her palm against the rock hard wall of his stomach, raising a brow. Sera bit her lip and tilted her head, flushing when she realized that she wanted to see them… all of them.

"Can we… wear less clothes? I want to see you," she admitted.

Two bright grins stunned her momentarily as the brothers both stripped off their shirts and jeans, torso muscles rippling with each little movement. Soon, they were clad in nothing but tight boxer briefs, white for Kieran and black for Kellan.

A funny reverse, she thought, *of the Light and the Dark*. God, they were beautiful to behold. The moment was lost when Kellan drew her to her feet and turned her, fingers brushing the nape of her neck as he brushed her hair over her shoulder and slowly unzipped her dress.

Two sets of hands peeled the dress from her body. One brother unclasped and removed her bra, the other slid her panties down her legs. Two sets of hands explored her bare back, her ass, her hips. She closed her eyes, inhaling a shaky breath as her two lovers cupped and squeezed her breasts, pinched and rolled her sensitive nipples.

"What do you like, Sera?" Kellan purred in her ear.

"I…" she started, shaking her head. She didn't know. It was too much. She wanted it all, every touch and stroke, every whisper against her skin… all at once, somehow.

"Turn around," Kieran told her, his big hands guiding her. The brothers shifted without speaking. Kellan sat on the edge of the bed and pulled Sera down to sit on his lap, facing Kieran as he stood before her. There was a practiced gentleness to their movements, as if they'd done this before, shared a partner just in this way, but Sera found she didn't mind.

All she could think of was the way Kellan's long, heavy cock pressed against her back. The way Kellan touched and teased her breasts as Kieran drew Sera's long curtain of hair out of the way, back over Kellan's shoulder. Kieran cupped Sera's jaw, the rough pad of his thumb grazing and pulling down her lower lip.

His manhood lay against his belly, thick and proud, and he reached down to stroke himself without breaking eye contact with her.

She arched her back, pressing her breasts harder into Kellan's touch as she darted her tongue out to brush Kieran's thumb. A low rumble escaped his throat, and Sera looked up at him with hooded eyes as she wrapped her lips around his thumb, drawing it into her mouth, sucking on it teasingly.

"Fuck, Sera," Kieran ground out. "Your mouth feels good.

Perfectly hot and wet. I can't wait to feel your delicious mouth wrapped around my cock while Kellan fucks your tight little pussy from behind."

Sera moaned, his dirty talk setting her aflame.

"Oh, you like that?" Kellan whispered in her ear, his lips against the sensitive skin of her neck making her shiver. "Mmmm, you are a bad girl, aren't you?"

Kellan's hand left her breast and trailed down, down until two thick fingers brushed her lower lips. Sera moaned and bucked her hips against him, desperate and hungry for more.

"I can't wait to taste you here," Kellan whispered, exploring her slick slit with his fingertips. "Right… here?"

He brushed her clit with the softest of strokes, and Sera couldn't help herself. She spread her knees apart, giving him greater access.

"Oh, you do like that, hm?" Kellan said. "Maybe my brother will give you a little of what you need, Sera."

Kellan pulled Sera back on the bed, still laying atop his body. His big hands kept her thighs parted, his lips moved over the nape her neck as he ground his heavy, hard cock against her ass cheeks. For a moment, Sera was confused.

Then Kieran dropped to his knees before them and buried his mouth against her aching sex, making her cry out.

"Oh! Yes! Yes!" was all she could manage.

Kieran's lips and tongue worked at her clit, driving her to the brink of insanity. When he slid two long fingers deep into her tight channel, Sera nearly screamed with the pleasure of it.

"He's got to get you ready so you can take my cock, darling," Kellan whispered, pinching and tugging her nipples until she thought she could die from want. "I want to fuck you harder than you've ever had in your life, and I want you to take all of it, and love it. This time, I'm just going to take that beautiful pussy while my brother fucks your mouth. But next time... next time we will take you together."

As Kellan said the last, Kieran pressed a fingertip against her rear entrance, working with a gentle but firm pressure until he could slide his finger deeper, deeper. The sensation overloaded every one of Sera's circuits, her orgasm ripping from her body almost painfully as she screamed her pleasure aloud.

Neither of her mates slowed down, not for a moment.

Kieran stood as Kellan sat up once more, supporting Sera's suddenly-heavy body. Sera let them control her, let Kellan turn her over so that she was on her hands and knees. Kellan positioned himself behind her, Kieran before her at the edge of the bed.

"Open your mouth, darling," Kieran said, his brogue thick as molasses.

Sera licked her lips, looking up at him as he fisted his thick cock and presented it to her. Keeping her lips and tongue soft and pliant, she glued her gaze to Kieran's as he fed his length into her mouth. He cupped the back of her head, adjusting the angle until she could take him deeper, a little at a time.

"Fuck, Sera. Your mouth... Gods, you feel good. I'm not going to last," he swore.

He moved in gentle strokes, guiding her movements, doing most of the work. Which was a good thing, because Sera felt Kellan grip her hips, rubbing the thick crown of his cock against her inner thigh. He nudged her knees apart, positioning himself at her aching entrance, then used his free hand to angle her hips just so.

He thrust deep, filling her body as thoroughly as Kieran filled her mouth and throat. Sera moaned, her body stretching pleasurably to accommodate his size.

"You like this, darling? Having two mates fucking you at

the same time, making you quiver, taking you hard?" Kellan asked.

To punctuate that, he began to move faster, harder. Sera's eyes nearly rolled up in her head as Kellan stroked into her already-sensitive flesh again and again. She wanted to call his name, to groan, but she could do nothing. She watched Kieran's expression, watched his body tighten, watched sweat break out over his whole body.

Her mates needed her like this, needed her body. Needed release.

And Sera wanted to give it to them.

Steadying herself on one hand, Sera reached out and put her free hand on Kieran's bare ass, drawing him in further. Encouraging him, driving him higher.

"Fuck!" he gritted out. His excitement made heat coil lower in Sera's body, the tension ramping up as Kellan reached around and pressed his fingers to her clit, massaging in slow circles.

Sera burst again, pleasure firing bright, her veins flooded with the sensation of her two mates fucking her at once. She was only vaguely aware of Kieran and Kellan tensing and crying out, both pulsing their seed deep inside her. She was too overloaded to know anything, too overfull of bliss and heat and wonder.

When Kieran and Kellan positioned her to kneel on the bed, each one on his knees beside her, she bit her lip.

"Mark me?" she asked, though she already knew they intended to do it.

Twin growls burst from their lips as Kieran and Kellan sunk their teeth into the soft skin at the base of her neck, one on each side. The pain was nothing compared to the glowing pleasure that bloomed in her chest, the feeling of connection that warmed her from the soul outward.

They collapsed in a sweaty, naked heap, kissing and

laughing and cuddling. No more needed to be said, just the pleasure of one another's company.

When Sera fell asleep, tucked between her two brawny alpha mates, she'd never felt quite so cherished in her whole life. More than that, even...

She felt more than desired. She felt *loved*.

CHAPTER 12

Sera left her two mates sleeping in Kellan's bed. Big though it was, the men dominated it. Sera found herself wondering whether they would keep up their current arrangement, each twin with his own room and Sera's in the middle. Would she go to one of them or the other depending on her whims, or would they always share her as they had tonight?

It remained to be seen. She padded down the hallway to her own room, conscious of her nakedness. She'd never seen another Guardian on this floor, but someone might see her from the stairs. The Guardians and their mates kept odd hours, someone was always coming or going, but tonight the whole Manor was quiet.

Sera's lips twitched when the thought occurred to her that the other Guardians might be trying to follow in Cassie and Gabriel's footsteps, have a baby of their own… and they might be starting right now, the old fashioned way. Shaking her head, she went into her bedroom and pulled on a pair of silk pajamas and a robe.

You just have sex on the brain, she told herself, but she probably wasn't too far off base. Looking at little baby Marie had stirred something in Sera's heart, not that her biological clock was any surprise. It had been ticking, and ticking loudly, for a few years now. The second she was done with her high-pressure medical residency, her body had been ready and willing.

She headed downstairs, her head in the clouds.

Now, she had everything she needed to succumb to her ticking clock. The Gray brothers were the final piece of Sera's puzzle. Not one, but two mates to cherish and provide for a baby. An image of Kieran and Kellan each holding a baby, a pair of twins just like themselves…

It turned Sera gooey inside, almost to an embarrassing degree.

"Daydreaming?"

Sera jumped, her hand flying to cover her heart. Duverjay stood in the kitchen, polishing a large pile of silverware.

"You scared me!" she said with an uncomfortable laugh. "Do you ever sleep?"

She cocked her head and examined the butler, who was still perfectly pressed and impressive in his conservative tuxedo. It was only then that Sera realized that though she had the vague impression that Duverjay was Kith, she didn't know precisely what kind he was.

Much like her own uncertain lineage, as a matter of fact.

"I do," he assured her. "I require much less than the average human, though. Just an hour or two during the afternoon, when the whole Manor is quiet."

"I gotcha," Sera said with a nod. "Well, I don't mean to disturb you. I just came down to look at a couple of the texts on the library wall down here, and maybe look up some stuff online."

"Very well. Would you like something to drink while you work? Coffee or tea?" Duverjay suggested.

Sera pursed her lips, then smiled.

"You wouldn't happen to have hot cocoa, would you?" she asked.

Duverjay's face split into a grin.

"Of course, my lady."

Sera tried not to roll her eyes at his formal address, thanking the butler and moving to the conference table. One corner of the meeting area boasted floor-to-ceiling wood bookshelves, crammed with reference books on all things magic. Sera took her time, scanning all the shelves and selecting a half-dozen tomes that she believed would be the most relevant to her research.

Duverjay brought over her hot cocoa, neatly arranged on a tray with some Danish butter cookies.

"You are a wicked man," she teased him, grinning when he turned to leave with a pleased smile.

Sera nibbled a cookie and sipped her decadent cocoa as she dove into the books she chose, flipping through the first without much luck. Tons of mentions of different creatures, a huge chunk dedicated to whatever the heck a *djinni* was, but nothing on phoenixes.

The second book at least had a beautifully illuminated photo of a phoenix, a stunning jewel-toned bird in a bright burst of blue flame. After scanning the information below, she quickly surmised that this wasn't what she was looking for. After all, she wasn't a damn bird, she was just…

A mystery.

Pushing the second book away with a sigh, she pushed on. The third and fourth were a bust, which frustrated her. Maybe she was crazy to be pursuing this based on the word of some old Kith man who hung out in the French Quarter all day. She didn't know him from Adam; he could have been making it all up.

The enthusiasm in his eyes, though… it had seemed genuine. Wrinkling her nose, Sera grabbed the fifth of her selections, a mammoth leather-bound book whose cover read *Mythes*. No other description, but it looked much older than most of the books in the Manor's small library, which was her reason for choosing it.

Unfortunately, when she flipped open the creaking brown leather cover, she discovered that the whole thing was in French. In fact, Sera had a sneaking suspicion that it wasn't even modern French, just going by the unfamiliar characters and the strange ways the words were clustered.

Sera groaned and shoved the book away, then pressed the heels of her hands against her eyes. She should just head back upstairs, try to get some sleep, forget this whole thing.

"Did you need assistance?" Duverjay asked, making Sera jump for the second time that night.

"Ah, no more cocoa," she said, dropping her hands and looking up at the butler, trying to keep her tone lighthearted. "And I'd love more cookies, but I don't want to have to run off all the calories tomorrow."

"As you wish, ma'am, but I was referring to the book," he said, pointing to *Mythes*.

"It's in French," Sera said.

"I know. It's my book," Duverjay said, arching a brow.

"You read ancient French?" she asked, her face heating. "I'm so sorry, I had no idea."

"It's Old French, actually, and yes. Is there something particular you're looking for?"

"Yes. I'm looking for any information about phoenixes. Not the birds," she added hastily. "The, um… beings. People."

Duverjay didn't comment, or even react.

"I think I have just the thing," he said, gesturing to the seat across from hers. "If I may."

"Of course, yes, please," she said. The servant-master thing still flustered her; it was something that she would perhaps never get used to. As a doctor she gave orders and ran important operations, but she also believed in acting as if she *served* her patients. After all, their well-being came first.

While she was busy mulling over the philosophical ramifications of having a butler on the Guardians' staff, Duverjay seated himself and sifted through the book's pages with great care.

"Ah, here we are," he announced. "The Phoenix."

He scanned the page for a long moment before beginning. Sera's heart began to beat a little faster, her mouth going dry. Curiosity gnawed at her insides.

"The phoenix is an immortal being who lives a thousand or more lives. They have existed since antiquity, the sons and daughters of the sons and daughters of the gods. Like many powerful creatures, they have been hunted nearly to extinction, prized for what they can give another. The phoenix's power is no common thing, as it only rises once every thirty years. In the thirtieth year of life, under the fullest moon, a phoenix will rise and change, opening portals to other realms and making many impossible things possible... but only while the phoenix is in-between rising and razing. Once the phoenix burns, they rise from the ashes, fully formed and grown but different than any person they've been before. Then, the cycle begins anew. Live, rise, burn, recur." He paused. "That's the end of the article, my lady."

Duverjay looked up from the text, then turned the book around and slid it over to Sera. There on the page was a sketch, the curved outline of a woman with her hands thrown up in the air, as if rejoicing. All around her were flames, but her expression was jubilant. No fear, no pain, no sorrow.

Radiance was the word that came to mind.

"Wow," was all Sera could think to say.

"Indeed." Duverjay rose and pushed his chair back into place, giving her a little bow. "Let me know if I can assist you further."

Mind whirling, Sera forced herself to open and examine the final book in painstaking detail, though it contained no information of value.

Thirty years. Fullest moon. Rise, change, burn...

She could barely process it, and once she had gone through all the information a few times, she wasn't sure what to *do* with what Duverjay had read to her. After all, it was a single centuries-old source, origin unknown. Depending on the precise age of the text, the people who wrote it might have also thought the Earth to be flat.

In addition to that, Sera had turned thirty nearly eight months ago. Her thirtieth year was nearly over, and surely in the eight moons she'd witnessed this year the fullest had already passed. Didn't that take place in the summer, like pagan fertility festivals and whatnot?

Sera couldn't remember. Still, she was sure it was just a superstition. She'd just need to keep researching, look for something to support or deny the claims of *Mythes*. Until then, any actions she took would just be grasping at straws and jumping at shadows.

"Duverjay?" she called as she rose and began to reshelve the books.

"Ma'am?" he said, appearing around the corner.

"Would it be all right if I asked you to keep this research between the two of us? I'm not quite sure what it means just yet." She bit her lip, trying to seem as innocuous as possible.

After a moment, he nodded.

"Of course, my lady."

"Thank you, Duverjay. I'm off to bed," she said, picking up her cocoa tray and handing it over to him.

"Sleep well, ma'am."

Sera nodded and gave him a brief smile, but it lacked warmth. What he suggested was impossible, with all these new ideas swimming around in her brain.

Sleep would be rare tonight, indeed.

CHAPTER 13

"Are Cassie and the baby all settled in?"

Sera looked up from her armful of research books to find Kieran waiting in the little sitting room they all shared. He dominated the plush chair he sat in, legs crossed as he sprawled, a determined set to his jaw.

Not a good sign, though Sera didn't know what he was upset about.

"They are," she said, dropping the armful of books on the room's only table. She walked over to the fireplace, glad that it was lit and roaring, and held out her hands to soak up some warmth.

Kellan strolled in, giving her an appreciative up-and-down glance. Still neither of her mates said anything. After a few more moments, it began to put Sera on edge.

"What?" she asked, turning to eye them both.

"I didn't say anything," Kellan drawled, but she could see that he had something on his mind.

"Just spit it out. What are you two conspiring about?"

Kellan snorted, but Kieran took the bait.

"We want you to take a longer leave from work," he said.

The words took the air out of Sera's mood, and she scowled at them both.

"No," she said simply.

"Sera..." Kellan started.

"You two are being ridiculous. All this talk of prophecies and danger, but none of it even seems real. I'm going back to work. Tomorrow, actually. I called and put myself in rotation."

Kieran rose, his posture a mirror of Kellan's equally hostile stance. Sera crossed her arms and squared off with them, unabashed.

"Don't," she said, pointing at both of them in turn. "You are my mates. You are not my keepers, or my daddies, or whatever. I am in charge of my own life, guys."

"Surely we have some say in matters of your safety, though," Kieran said, his frustration evident. "You can't just—"

"Stop right there. It's been almost a month since you guys brought me here. I've played nice, stayed here in the Manor, let you set the course. It's been too long. As a matter of fact, I got a message from my landlord asking me to come move my car, which has just been sitting on the street this whole time."

"And did you give him notice, like we talked about?" Kellan asked.

"I did. I have a few weeks to move things, but I am going over there now to get some of my more important mementos. And some better work clothes, since all I seem to have here are designer dresses."

"They look great on you," Kellan replied with a shrug, his eyes traveling up and down her body, admiring the clingy gray sweater dress she wore.

"Not practical for working shifts in the emergency room, though."

"So don't," Kieran said, but she could tell he was teasing

now. He reached out and snagged her hand, pulling her close to him, almost into his lap. "Can you wait until tomorrow to go to your apartment? That way one of us can go with you. Besides, I can think of better ways to spend our time before we go on patrol."

Kieran ran a finger from her collarbone to the tip of her breast, through her bra and dress, and Sera shivered. Kellan moved closer, one of his big hands closing around her hip, giving her a gentle squeeze.

"Mmmmm," she said, shaking her head even as Kellan kissed the nape of her neck. Kieran's fingers brushed her inner thigh just at her knee, traveling up, up, up... "Guys, no. We all have things to do. After your patrol, that's a whole different thing. But right now I'm all business."

She pulled away from them, trying not to blush when she saw the heated desire in their gazes.

"Tonight," she promised, unable to keep a smile from her lips. "And you two are going to be late for patrol if you don't leave now."

Kieran and Kellan shared a glance.

"Fine," Kellan said, shaking his head. "But I don't like this."

Kieran only scowled.

"You don't have to," Sera said, keeping her tone light. "Everything is going to be fine. Let's all walk downstairs together."

She parted ways with her mates at the Manor's front doors, heading out front. She pulled out her phone and hailed an Uber, passing a quiet ride to her MidCity apartment.

Once there, she managed to pack all her necessities and put the boxes she'd loaded in her car in less than two hours. Looking around at the rest of her furniture in her strangely bare apartment, she pursed her lips. What to do with the rest of it? Maybe she should hire movers and just put everything in storage, for now.

But if that was just for now, what would come later? The Manor wasn't her home, not in a long-term sense. She was embarrassed to realize that she hadn't put any real thought into the situation, much less talked to Kieran and Kellan about their future plans beyond the Guardians. Simply put, she'd been too drunk on love and sex to spend a lot of time thinking *any* of it through. So unlike her!

Mulling that thought over, Sera headed out of the apartment and locked up. She crossed the street, heading for her car, running down her to-do list in her head. She'd just hit the unlock button on her key fob when she heard the screech of tires.

Turning her head, she saw a white van fly around the corner of the quiet side street where she was parked. Sera flattened herself against her car, thinking that the driver was drunk or perhaps lost control of the vehicle.

When it skidded to a halt only feet from her, Sera turned and scrambled to open her door. The sliding door began to open, and her heart pounded in response. She had no idea what was happening, only that something was very, very wrong. She'd just managed to get into the car when a dark-robed figure ripped the car door clear off its hinges and reached inside to grasp Sera's arm.

It took three of the faceless, monk-like assailants to drag her from her car. Sera screamed at the top of her lungs, and she even saw someone pass by on the street, turning to watch, what was apparently, her abduction. The stranger pulled out a cell phone, but Sera lost track of him.

A dark piece of cloth was thrust over her head, her hands bound too. Then her attackers picked her up and tossed her in the van as easily as a bag of garbage. Her head smashed against something, hard, and the fight went out of her.

Never let them take you to a second location, rang in her head, the advice useless.

Her head ached, and for a moment she thought she might be sick. She closed her eyes and took deep breaths, trying not to react when a set of ice-cold fingers brushed her neck, checking her pulse.

Let them think you're unconscious, she told herself. *It's the only advantage you can give yourself right now.*

Forcing herself to relax, Sera focused on listening to everything around her, trying to take in as much detail about her surroundings as possible. In short order, the van stopped, and she was lifted and carried once more.

After a minute of bouncing around as she laid across someone's shoulders like a sack of potatoes, Sera's butt landed on a metal chair. Cold hands leaned her back, positioning her hands and attaching them to the chair with metal cuffs.

Then, silence. For a long time, Sera heard nothing but the sound of her own breathing. Her heart thrummed in her chest, and soon she felt a tear slip down her left cheek.

This was the bad thing Cassie had prophesied. On the very day she'd told her mates to quit worrying, to let her be independent, *it* was happening. What had Cassie said, exactly?

Ripped apart.

Sera shuddered, a quiet whimper escaping her lips.

"Ah, you're awake," came a deep bass voice. Thickly accented, exotic. French, but more than that. "Uncover her."

The dark cloth bag was yanked off her head, leaving her to wince in the bright afternoon light. She sat in a big, abandoned warehouse of some sort, sunlight streaming in through patchy holes in the roof.

A tall, almost skeletal man stood before her, his ebony skin gleaming. His eyes were sunken to dark hollows, though the whites were shockingly light. His smile, too, was so white it nearly glowed. He wore an impeccably-tailored white suit, complete with a blood-red tie and pocket square and wing-tip shoes.

"There, that's better," he said, almost to himself.

"Who are you?" Sera blurted out, wincing at the volume of her own voice. Her head still throbbed, and everything sounded a little too loud.

"Who am I?" he asked with a grin. "Papa Aguiel, of course. Surely your friends the Guardians have told you about me, little bird."

Now that she watched him speak, Sera was pretty sure that his accent was Haitian. From what little she knew of Papa Aguiel, gathered from the other Guardians' mates and a few midnight research sessions, Haitian would make sense.

The man watched her for a few moments, as if assessing her. He walked around her in a wide circle, looking her up and down. Something about the way he walked suggested that he was hiding a limp; his sunken cheeks and glassy eyes made Sera think he was sick.

Could one such as Papa Aguiel, a Vodun Loa somehow come to life, *be* sick?

"Yes, you will do," he said. Again, he seemed to be talking to himself as much as her. "I thought you'd hide through the full moon, and ruin it for me… When I heard you were in the Gray Market, flaunting your two Guardian mates… Surely, I thought, she is lost to me now."

Sera didn't reply. She only watched him with what she hoped was a stoic expression. He chuckled and ran his hands down the front of his suit.

"Yet here you are, little bird. A phoenix, the one creature who can keep me in the mortal realm forever. What a beautiful Vessel you are, Serafina."

"What the hell are you talking about?" Sera said, her

curiosity overcoming her unwillingness to participate. Papa Aguiel continued as if she had not spoken.

"When I possess your body, you will fit me like a glove. While I conquer and rule the human realm, I think you will be there, too. Inside, somewhere." He cocked his head as if listening to some secret sound. "Sometimes I can hear this Vessel, the one I possess now, deep down inside. Screaming, mostly. I hope you will not scream so much as this one, Serafina."

Sera's mouth dropped open, but she had no answer for that. Her whole body began to tremble as she worked out the meaning of his words. *Possess... Vessel... screaming...*

Gods, he meant to take over her body? Apparently it wouldn't be the Loa's first time, either.

"Truly, you will be luckier than you know," he told her, his tone cool and conversational, like they were two strangers on the streetcar talking about weather. "You will see it all firsthand. The rivers running with blood, the skies weeping black. The human race falling to their knees, surrendering to their new master... Yes, it will be a sight to behold. And you, dear Serafina, you will make it all possible."

"Me?" Sera asked, flinching. "Why me?"

"Because you are the last phoenix, and the only creature powerful enough to act as my Vessel and hold my shape forever. On this full moon, you will rise and burn, shed your form. In that moment, I will take your place, complete my final form."

He paused, then looked directly in Sera's eyes.

"It will be spectacular."

With that, he spun on his heel and left her, bound and aghast.

Sera let her head hang down, unable to lift a finger to save her own life.

CHAPTER 14

Kieran glanced up from the grimy cobblestones lining Pirate's Alley in the French Quarter, giving Kellan a once-over. His brother was uncharacteristically silent as they wrapped up their night's patrol a little early. It was nearly eleven p.m., and the whole Quarter was suspiciously still under the foggy, moonlit sky. Even the human tourists seemed restrained, almost sleepy. Usually when the first night of the full moon fell on a weekend night, as was the case tonight, all the loonies and drunks and were-creatures came out in full force and wreaked havoc.

"Even Pirate's Alley is empty? I'll be damned," Kieran said, shaking his head. "I've never seen a full moon as tame as this one."

"I don't like it," was Kellan's only response.

Kieran nodded. He felt heavy, like he'd gone through a full-length battle… except they hadn't so much as vanquished a demon. In the back of his mind, too, was the gnawing worry over Sera. She'd called him paranoid, but Kieran just *felt* like something was going to go wrong. That gut instinct had saved him a thousand times over by now, and he tried to listen to it as best he could.

If only he could pinpoint the issue, the exact thing that worried him. This general unease and dragging worry was unlike him.

When Kellan yawned and suggested grabbing coffee on the way back to the Manor, something clicked into place for Kieran.

"It's a spell," Kieran said, resisting the urge to smack himself in the forehead.

"What?" Kellan asked, smothering another yawn.

"That," Kieran said, pointing straight up. "The fog. It's a spell. That's why we're both tired and anxious, why there's hardly anyone out in the streets tonight. Someone wants everyone to stay in tonight, mind their own business. Stay out of the way, more like."

"Gods, you're right," Kellan said. "I can't believe I didn't see it."

"I think that might be part of the spell, too." Kieran squinted up at the thin, misty fog. "It's very cleverly made. That's what worries me most."

"We need to get back to the Manor," Kellan said. "There was a police car idling on the last block, let's go back and hail a ride from the officer."

Kieran nodded and followed Kellan's lead. After flashing their Guardian IDs to the officer, they got the fastest of rides back home.

"Thank you, officer," Kieran said when they hopped out in front of the Manor.

"Night, gentlemen," the cop said, dipping his head. For the briefest moment, the officer's irises blazed bright yellow, his subtle way of outing himself as Kith.

"Stay alert tonight," Kieran said. "Something's going down, though I don't know what."

The officer gave him a salute, then pulled off.

"Kieran!" Kellan stood in the front doorway, waiting for his twin to jog up to meet him. "Sera didn't come home tonight."

"Did you try calling her?" Kieran asked.

His twin nodded. "No response."

"Fuck."

"Hey, there you guys are," Echo said from the foyer. "Come inside, I need to talk to you both."

Kieran and Kellan stepped inside, all ears to see what Rhys's mate had up her sleeve.

"Mere Marie said you were looking for Sera," Echo said. "Which is funny, because I just got a tip-off about her. I've been grooming this Gray Market security guy as an informant for a while now, and he just left me a message. He got hired for an outside job, working security on a private contract. Working for some creepy Haitian guy, he says. Sound familiar?"

"What about Sera?" Kellan asked, frustration heavy in his voice.

"Right, sorry. The guard said he met Sera a while ago, saw her hanging out with you guys in the Gray Market. Apparently the job he's working involves holding a captive, and the lady they're guarding looks a hell of a lot like Sera. Apparently the boss is shelling out big for this job, too."

"We have to check it out, at least," Kieran said.

"Did Echo fill you in?" Rhys asked, coming up to join them.

"Yeah. Why aren't you all suited up and ready?" Kellan asked.

"We've fallen into this trap before, sending all the Guardians to one location and leaving the Manor and the rest of the city unprotected," Rhys sighed. "Gabriel and I are going to stay here and hold down the fort. Asher and Aeric are going to go with you to check out the situation. The address Echo's informant gave us is just up the road in the seventh ward, so we can reach you easily if needed. Or vice versa," Rhys explained.

Asher strode into the foyer, Aeric close on his heels.

"We're ready. Duverjay's waiting in the parking deck for us," Aeric said, nodding toward the back of the house. "We need to roll on this, right now. It's only half an hour until midnight, and there's a reason they call it the witching hour. That's when shit goes down."

"Agreed. We'll grab some more ammo on the way out," Kellan said.

The men rolled out, promising Rhys that they'd stay in constant contact. After a hair-raising drive into a half-abandoned neighborhood that Kieran had never visited, they pulled up and got out on a block of crumbling, abandoned warehouses.

"Right there, on the left," Asher said, pointing. "467 Port."

"Funny seeing reinforced steel doors on a place that looks like half the roof is caved in," Kieran said.

"We should go around the side, breach through a window," was Aeric's suggestion.

They moved on silent feet down a dark, tight side alley. Kellan spotted a window that was already missing a pane of glass, and gestured to everyone to ready themselves. Kieran held up a hand, asking them to wait. He placed his bare palm against the remaining glass and froze it solid, which would make their entrance a little safer.

Asher boosted Kellan up and Kellan busted through the window as quietly as possible, then disappeared inside. Kieran followed next, with Asher and Aeric right behind him. When Kieran's feet hit the scuffed cement floor of the huge empty space, he spotted Sera immediately.

In fact, she was impossible to miss.

At the far end of the warehouse, two figures stood. One was a dark-skinned man in a suit, which could only be Papa Aguiel. The other figure was standing on what looked like a stone altar, head thrown back and arms spread wide. Sera.

And she was *glowing*. Bright, blinding white, with vivid blue outlining her form. Her hair was a curtain of black flame, and she wore a thin white ceremonial robe that flowed over her curvy body like pristine, silken water.

Between the Guardians and Sera were at least two dozen black-robed Vodun priests, and they were already moving to attack.

Even from here, Kieran could feel the heat radiating off her.

"Phoenix," he heard Aeric whisper. "I thought they were all extinct."

"Let's move," Kellan said, surging forward.

"Wait! She's going to burn, there's no way we can stop that," Aeric said. "She's going to shed her form. I don't know what Papa Aguiel has planned, but we have to focus on stopping him and keeping him from whatever he wants to do."

"What about Sera?" Kieran asked.

"I'm sorry, I don't... I don't know," Aeric said, drawing his sword.

The sound of steel rung out in the heavy, silent air as the Guardians pulled their weapons and faced off against Papa Aguiel's henchmen. Though it only took a few minutes for Kieran and the other Guardians to fight their way through most of the assailants, it seemed they were out of time.

"Too late!" Papa Aguiel crowed, holding up a small black object. A remote? "It's midnight. Time to watch the pretty little bird burn."

He pressed a button and a panel in the ceiling slid back, pouring moonlight down onto the altar where Sera stood.

She cried out as her whole body burst into fierce white flame, engulfing her in an orb of dazzling, burning white light. Just as Kieran got close, Papa Aguiel looked right at the Guardians, laughed, and stepped into the fire.

He vanished.

"Shit!" Kieran shouted. He could feel Kellan right beside him as they both rushed headlong into the fire. First, he felt a burst of scalding heat.

Then, nothingness.

CHAPTER 15

Kellan held his breath as he fell through white nothingness for several heart-pounding moments. Then suddenly, he was plunged into near darkness, his feet almost going out from under him when he hit the soft, loamy ground. It was nearly pitch-dark, the only illumination coming from a creeping gray mist that swirled through the air, clinging to his limbs and sticking in his lungs. He could hear a strange sound, like the ticking of a clock, or a faint heartbeat; it reverberated through the whole plane, skittering across his skin.

The worst part of it all was the complete, utter silence, like being in a total vacuum.

When Kieran's hand landed on his arm, Kellan jumped.

Look, his twin mouthed. The word sounded in his mind instead out loud, which was jarring. Kieran gave Kellan an impatient look and wrenched him around to face the opposite direction.

Kellan's mouth fell open. There, a hundred yards away, was a massive column of gray-and-white flickering fire. Even as he watched, it grew and grew, burning higher and brighter. Inside the column was Sera, her mouth open in a silent scream of agony, black tears rolling down her cheeks as she burned.

Get her out of there, I'll get the bad guy, Kieran said, moving toward Papa Aguiel, who was on the other side of Sera, staring at her with a strange expression of glee.

Kellan started moving toward Sera, then frowned. Moving was nearly impossible, like trying to walk through freshly poured concrete. It took all his strength just to make it close enough to get Sera's attention. She pressed her hands against the wall of flame, looking as if she were trapped behind a wall of glass, a fresh bout of tears running down her face.

Her mouth moved, and her voice slithered through his mind.

You can't be here. You will burn, she said. Though Sera was clearly panicked and in pain, her voice in his head was cool and calm. For some reason, that made Kellan furious. What the fuck was this horrible place?

The flames around her flared and jumped higher, higher. Kellan's whole body broke into a fierce sweat. He pushed forward two more steps, and he could feel the heat licking his skin, feel the hair on his arms begin to curl.

"What do I do?" he shouted.

Sera clawed at the flames, shaking her head, anger in her eyes. Like she really expected her mates to just leave her, abandon her to... whatever the hell was going on here?

Fuck no.

Out of the corner of his eye, Kellan saw Papa Aguiel shove Kieran away, sending his sword spinning off into the mist. Papa Aguiel grinned and started dragging himself toward Sera with a single-minded sort of determination, and suddenly Kellan realized... the guy was going to try to get *in* the flames with her.

A long, keening scream echoed through Kellan's mind, and he glanced back at Sera. He could see that she was beginning to fade, the lines of her body growing harder to distinguish from the rest of the flame.

She's going to burn out, he thought. *Maybe... maybe if I get inside? Or Kieran can use his magic to cool her off...*

Something shifted into place into his brain. She was burning. She would fade, and die. Kieran had the power of icy death, Kellan the power of fresh life...

They could save her, but it would take both of them at once to do it.

There was a shout of pain from Papa Aguiel, and a victorious sound from Kieran. Kellan saw that his twin had plunged a long black dagger into the other man's chest, and now Papa Aguiel staggered backward, trying to get away.

"Leave him!" Kellan shouted, seeing Kieran wince at the way Kellan's words rang in his mind. "We have to go into the fire, together!"

You can't save her, fools, Papa Aguiel's voice hissed. *You can't tame the phoenix. She has risen, she burns. Now she must die and be reborn. It is their way.*

When Kieran bared his teeth at Papa Aguiel, the villain only shook his head.

You will die. I will find another way, he promised, turning and vanishing from view.

"Now, Kieran!" Kellan cried.

They both waded toward each other, Kellan reaching out and grabbing his twin's hand, gripping it like a lifeline. Somehow, having Kieran so close made it easier to move, easier to breathe. They walked right up to Sera, then glanced at one another.

"We have to keep her from burning. You use your magic first, cool and dark. Then I use mine, bright and warm. We can save her, brother," Kellan told Kieran.

Kieran nodded, understanding dawning in his expression.

No! Sera screeched when they started to move into the flames. *Turn back! Turn back!*

Jaw set, Kellan summoned an orb of his magic into one hand, holding up a bright white ball before his eyes. Beside him, Kieran held an identical orb in pitch black.

Life. Death.

Salvation.

Nodding at one another, they both thrust their hands into the fire. It was everything he could do not to jerk his hand back. Kellan opened the font of power deep within himself, unleashing it and pushing it out through his hand. The fire caught and danced across his skin wildly, and he felt a tug low in his body. The fire pulled at his power, drawing it out of him, draining him of everything, inside and out.

Making him empty and dim.

Still, he didn't dare stop.

The fire burned, ripped at his flesh, made him scream with agony.

And he didn't stop. Even when he felt Kieran's fingers burning, searing his own, he did not stop.

For Sera, he gave everything…

Even when that meant surrendering to the flames, letting himself turn to ash and float away on the wind…

Kellan let go.

CHAPTER 16

Sera had never been quite so sore in her whole life. She peeled her eyes open, wrinkling her nose at the stiffness in her limbs. She felt so *heavy*.

Which could be explained by the two big alpha males, sprawled protectively over her body, even in their sleep. Arms criss-crossing her body, Kieran and Kellan each had their face pressed against the top of her head. She was in a human cocoon of safety and warmth.

Tears pricked her eyes. Sera drew in a deep breath, the memories of their trip to the warehouse rushing back. How they'd saved her, risked their lives for her, protected her to the bitter end.

And then, unbidden, more memories started to come back. Beyond her time with Kieran and Kellan. Beyond med school, high school, childhood.

Back to her past lives. In the blink of an eye, all her memories were there. It was like an ocean of diamonds in her mind, each facet a bittersweet memory of a life she'd lived, a person she'd known and loved, a self she'd lost when she rose and burned as the Phoenix.

Only this time... this time, somehow, her mates had stopped the transition. Kept her from leaving her body and mind behind, broken the cycle that she might have repeated for a thousand more lifetimes.

They'd saved her in more ways than they could possibly understand. More than she could even try to explain, for now at least.

Now... now she just wanted to thank them, kiss them, hold them.

"Um... guys?" Sera croaked.

They both opened their eyes, staring at her as if in disbelief.

"Fuck," Kieran growled, dragging her up to his lips for a kiss. Hard, desperate, needy. "Fuck, Sera. It's been a week. We thought you'd never wake."

"Come here," Kellan said, twining his arms around her waist.

Sera turned her face to his and got another fierce, emotional lip lock. Kieran's lips touched her collarbone, making her shiver. Already his hands roamed her body, tugging at her nightgown, pulling her soft body against his hard, muscular form.

"I remember," she whispered against Kellan's lips. "I remember it all now... I've lived a thousand lives, lost a thousand loves... until you."

She sighed as Kellan cupped her breasts, ran his tongue over her lower lip.

"You saved me," she finished, trying not to tear up.

"We'd do anything for you," Kieran whispered.

"We will give you everything, Sera. Everything."

Kellan pressed against her, sandwiching Sera's body between her two mates.

"Everything?" she asked.

"Everything," Kieran affirmed.

"A family?" she asked.

Both of her mates chuckled as they kissed her sensitive skin, sending a chill of pleasure straight down her spine.

"Fuck yes. We're going to start right now," Kellan said with a grin.

"We're going to have our way with you, Sera. Take turns. And we're not leaving this bedroom until you get what you want," Kieran promised with a matching smirk.

"What have I got myself into?" Sera asked with a laugh, which quickly turned breathless as Kieran stripped off her nightgown.

The question didn't need an answer, though. It was all too obvious.

She'd gotten herself into bed and into love with the two most perfect men in existence.

I'm the luckiest woman in the world, she thought. *Plain and simple.*

EPILOGUE

Mere Marie stood in her bedroom at the Manor, staring out the window. Part of the magic of the Manor was that she could add floor after floor to the place, raise it higher and higher as she added new fighters to her little brood. Since her room was at the top, the view from her bedroom window only got better and better.

And since the place was glamoured to resemble a two-story mansion rather than the rambling multi-story monster it really was, Mere Marie never heard a word of complaint from the neighborhood association.

Perfection.

She sipped her chicory root tea, watching lighting strike wildly across the city skyline.

Something was happening tonight, more than just the Gray brothers rescuing their mate.

Something big.

Papa Aguiel was making himself known, not bothering to hide whatever massive piece of magic he was working somewhere across the city. The lightning was part of that,

Mere Marie was certain. She wasn't certain how to move against her new enemy, though.

If she were honest with herself, the villain who'd somehow destroyed Pere Mal frightened her. Every time she tried to plot his downfall, her fingers began trembling. Strange, because Mere Marie feared almost nothing... except the big guys, heaven and hell, archangels and archdemons.

Here on good old Earth, she was used to being the scariest thing around.

Papa Aguiel, though... contemplating him made her hair stand on end.

She heard a noise in the distance, and this time it was more than just thunder. She put her teacup down and rushed out to the stairs. Below, she could see the Guardians and their mates heading downstairs. In the foyer, someone threw open the front door.

Mere Marie fairly flew down the stairs.

I knew it. I knew something was about to happen, she thought.

"How the heck did he even get into the yard? What about the Manor's wards?" Kira asked.

Mere Marie hit the ground floor and stalked over to the doorway, gently moving the woman out of her way.

There in the doorway was the crumpled, unconscious form of a big man. Rain soaked him through and through and his dark hair clung to his skull.

"Turn him over," Mere Marie commanded Asher, who stood right beside his mate.

Ever the obedient soldier, Asher reached out and turned over the stranger. Mere Marie's breath stuck in her throat, her fingers began to tremble again. The man roused for a moment, struggling against Asher's hands.

"Sophie? Is Sophie here yet?"

"Relax, man," Asher said.

The guy slumped back to the ground, his eyes rolling up in his head.

"Everyone move back!" Sera hollered. "We don't just leave unconscious people laying in the rain, guys."

She pushed her way through and checked his pulse, then touched his neck and checked him over.

"Can you guys get him into the living room, on one of the couches?" Sera asked, though her expression made it clear that she wasn't making a request.

Normally, Mere Marie's lips would have twitched with humor. Right now, though, they were numb.

"We can't just let a stranger in the house," Gabriel growled, moving to stop Kellan and Kieran from doing their mate's bidding.

"He is no stranger," Mere Marie said, clearing her throat.

Everyone turned to look at her.

"This is Ephraim," she said, glancing at the new man again. "He is the final Guardian."

Kieran and Kellan glanced at each other, shrugged, and went about getting Ephraim off the ground.

"What does this mean?" Alice asked, moving forward and patting Mere Marie's hand.

"He brings about the final battle and will ultimately decide the fate of all the Guardians," Mere Marie said, subconsciously rubbing her hand over her heart.

"That guy?" Echo asked, doing a double take. "He's a big deal?"

Mere Marie gave a slow nod. It was time that they all knew just how vital the coming days would be.

"He could save us all... or damn us, and let humanity fall to its knees."

Silence.

After all, what more was there to say?

GET A FREE BOOK!

JOIN MY MAILING LIST TO BE THE FIRST TO KNOW OF NEW RELEASES, FREE BOOKS, SPECIAL PRICES AND OTHER AUTHOR GIVEAWAYS.

http://freeshifterromance.com

ALSO BY KAYLA GABRIEL

Alpha Guardians

See No Evil

Hear No Evil

Speak No Evil

Bear Risen

Bear Razed

Bear Reign

ABOUT THE AUTHOR

Kayla Gabriel lives in the wilds of Minnesota where she swears she sees shifters in the woods beyond her yard. Her favorite things in life are mini marshmallows, coffee and when people use their blinker.

Connect with Kayla by
email: kaylagabrielauthor@gmail.com and be sure to get her FREE book: freeshifterromance.com

http://kaylagabriel.com

www.ingramcontent.com/pod-product-compliance
Lightning Source LLC
LaVergne TN
LVHW011843060526
838200LV00054B/4150